"I have a sister, Bryan."

He shrugged. "Lots of people have sisters."

Danni took a deep breath, steeling herself. "A twin sister. You've...you've met her."

He was getting the picture now. She could see it in his eyes. But his expression was unreadable. She would have preferred his anger, his outrage.

She didn't know how long they would've remained like this, frozen in a dreadful tableau. But then the front door opened, and heels clicked across the oak floor.

"Bryan? Bryan, I hope you're here—" Kristine appeared in the arch to the living room. And then she, too, froze as she glanced from Bryan to Danni and back again. Bryan faced them both.

Identical twin sisters!

Dear Reader,

What would it be like to have a twin? That's something I've often asked myself. I'm very close to my two sisters, but I can't help wondering what it would be like to have an identical twin. Would I find the similarities comforting? Or would I rebel against them?

These are the questions I've explored while writing *Christmas Babies*. Danni Ferris has tried as hard as she can to establish her own identity, her own life. But sibling closeness—and sibling rivalry—keep getting in the way. Especially when Danni and her identical twin sister fall in love with the same man…

I hope you enjoy reading Danni's story—and meanwhile I wish you a joyful holiday season!

Sincerely,

Ellen James

Christmas Babies

Ellen James

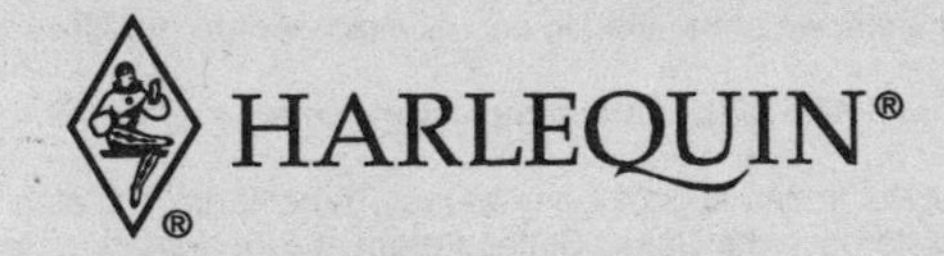

TORONTO • NEW YORK • LONDON
AMSTERDAM • PARIS • SYDNEY • HAMBURG
STOCKHOLM • ATHENS • TOKYO • MILAN • MADRID
PRAGUE • WARSAW • BUDAPEST • AUCKLAND

ISBN 0-373-70953-6

CHRISTMAS BABIES

This edition published by arrangement with Harlequin Books S.A.

Visit us at www.eHarlequin.com

Printed in U.S.A.

Christmas Babies

CHAPTER ONE

THE MAN WAS even more attractive than Danni had remembered. Dark brown eyes, darker hair...decisive features, a look of unassailable confidence. Bryan McKay also gave the impression that he appreciated the humor in a situation. Right now he was gazing at Danni with the faintest of smiles.

"You work fast," he said.

She flushed. Maybe she *was* being a little overenthusiastic. There'd been no answer when she'd knocked at Bryan's half-open door. And so she had wandered inside his house, started to get familiar with the place. A few moments later he'd appeared and found her in this rather awkward position, kneeling on the floor of the living room, her tape measure skittering out across the baseboard. She became uncomfortably aware of her less than professional appearance—windblown hair, denim shirt, canvas shorts, work boots. Ordinarily she met clients wearing a suit and heels. But today's business...well, it wasn't ordinary.

Danni had first seen Bryan a few months ago, when she'd joined Partner to Partner, a volunteer association of San Diego executives. Since then they'd had a few casual conversations at luncheons, charity dinners and the like. Bryan had mentioned the house he'd recently purchased, and its need for remodeling. Danni had mentioned her longtime dream of doing exactly that—remodeling a house with her own two hands. Of course, she'd told Bryan, her advertising career left no time for dreams. He'd told her not to be so sure. And then last week—unexpectedly—he'd called her, proposing this meeting. Maybe Danni could take on Bryan's house. They would discuss the idea, anyway.

"I guess I got ahead of myself," she admitted now, reeling in her tape measure. "It's just that ever since my Grandpa Daniel taught me how to use a miter saw, I've wanted to do some *real* carpentry work."

Bryan merely stood there watching her, his gaze lingering. She couldn't deny that she'd been attracted to him during their brief encounters in the past.

''I'm sure,'' Danni said, ''what you really want is a professional contractor—''

''First rule,'' Bryan said. ''Don't sell yourself short. Didn't they teach you that in advertising school?''

Danni grimaced. ''It would be different if I were trying to sell you on an ad campaign—''

''Because it wouldn't matter to you nearly as much,'' he interrupted.

The insight surprised her, and unsettled her, too. ''I guess we should discuss specifics,'' she said, trying to sound brisk. But suddenly Bryan walked toward her, took her hand and drew her up beside him. He had an air of knowing what he wanted. And his eyes seemed to say that right now he wanted *her.*

''Ridiculous,'' Danni muttered under her breath. Why was her imagination suddenly running away with her? She was usually very levelheaded.

''You are beautiful,'' he murmured now. She felt an odd sense of unease, small details intruding on the edge of her consciousness: the warm breeze stirring through the open window beside her, the dusty surface of the oak floors...the look in the man's eyes. Bryan drew her toward him, and then he put his arms around her and kissed her.

It was a firm kiss, a taking of possession kiss, his lips sending delight to the contours of hers. Her first instinct was, of course, to push him away. Yet somehow she found herself leaning toward him…leaning into him, a swirl of sensations catching her off guard. Desire, longing, confusion…

Impossible. This couldn't be happening. A man's arms, a man's touch…a man she hardly knew, making her feel as if she had come alive more than at any time she could remember.

Something thudded to the floor. It took Danni a few seconds to realize that she'd dropped her tape measure. She pulled away from him at last. He smiled at her. Perhaps the kiss had ended, but his eyes held a promise of more.

"I've been waiting to do that all day," he said.

"All day…?"

"After last night, Danni, I've been waiting." He took her into his arms again. But now Danni understood his words—and his actions—all too well. She felt a coldness deep inside, and then she just felt angry. There was only one explanation for this sexy, magical moment.

Kristine.

''I DON'T SEE WHY you're so upset. It's only a game, Danni. The same one we've always played,'' Kristine remarked several hours later.

Danni scowled at her twin sister, studying the face so much like her own she might as well have been looking into a mirror: blue-green eyes, a mouth just a shade too generous, a high forehead resolutely undisguised. In college Kristine and Danni had gone through a phase where they'd tried to minimize their foreheads with bangs. Kristine had been the one finally to let her blond hair grow out. Danni, as usual, had followed her sister's lead. But she was no longer the follower.

''We're a little old for that joke, don't you think?'' she said acidly. ''Switching places, trying to fool everyone we can. Dammit, Kris, you told him you were *me*. Used *my* name—''

''Well, I couldn't very well use my own, could I? After all, I'm a married woman. Supposedly, anyway.'' Kristine used her flippant tone, but she couldn't quite hide the misery shadowing her expression. Danni felt an unwilling stir of sympathy. Some things apparently didn't change: the way she hated to see Kristine unhappy for any reason, the fierce protectiveness she'd always felt toward her sister.

"I wish you'd tell me what's wrong between you and Ted," Danni said. "What's the real problem here?"

Kristine glanced away. "Ted is just...Ted. Nothing to be done about him. That's what Mom always says, anyway."

Kristine had committed the ultimate heresy in the Ferris clan—she'd married a lawyer instead of becoming one. According to the family view, it was mandatory for the Ferris girls to achieve success on their own. They weren't supposed to drop out of college one semester before graduation, meander from one job to another and then elope with a scandalously wealthy man ten years their senior. But that was exactly what Kristine had done.

"All right, forget Ted for now," Danni muttered, the anger washing over her again. "Let's discuss Bryan McKay instead. Let's talk about the fact that no matter what's going on in your marriage, you have no excuse for using *my* name, *my* identity to...what? Have an affair? He talked about last night as if..." Danni couldn't finish.

"Relax. It hasn't gone that far. Not for lack of wishing, though." Kristine drew up her knees and clasped her arms around them. She looked like a woman contemplating adultery.

Danni sank down on Kristine's sofa, the one upholstered in wild geometric shapes. It was like Kristine herself—vivid, excessive, yet rigidly structured.

"All right," Danni said, "you'd better tell me the whole story from the beginning. And don't leave anything out."

Kristine made an attempt at a careless shrug. "Surely you've figured it out by now. A couple of weeks ago, when you said you couldn't make that big event because you were too busy…I went in your place. It seemed harmless enough at the time. I needed…I needed something to forget my *own* life.… I told myself it would only be for a few hours. An escape for just a little while. But then this perfectly gorgeous man came up to me, and he thought I was you…and I didn't know how to tell him otherwise.…"

Danni remembered telling Kristine about the Partner to Partner gala, and how sorry she was that she couldn't attend. She'd never imagined, though, that her sister would use the opportunity to play the old game. It was the kind of thing Kristine had been guilty of at twelve, or sixteen.

Trying to escape whatever trouble she'd been in at the moment…pretending she was Danni. She ought to have outgrown that tactic long ago.

"How many times have you seen Bryan?"

"It doesn't really matter, does it?" Kristine mumbled.

"How many times, Kris?"

"Hardly any. The night I met him. And then twice afterward, if you count last night." Kristine was starting to get her defiant look—the one she always got when she realized she'd gone too far but wouldn't admit it. "I didn't plan on any of this, you know."

"Nothing you could do about it, I'm sure," Danni remarked sarcastically. "It was totally out of your control."

"Don't be so damned superior," Kristine snapped back. "*You* know why we've switched places before. It's a chance to slip out of your own life and into something more…bearable."

Admittedly, there had been times growing up when Danni had played the game, too. She'd longed to be someone more daring and reckless and so she'd pretended to be Kristine. But they were both adults now, thirty years old, and the time for pretending was long past.

Now Danni studied her sister. "Is your life

really so bad,'' she asked, ''that you have to escape?''

Kristine stood and moved to the impressive row of picture windows. Night had fallen, but the moon cast a glimmer on the beach and rippled across the ocean waves beyond.

''What could be bad?'' she asked, her voice hollow. ''Everyone thinks I have the most wonderful husband in the world.''

''Kris, what *is* going on with you and Ted?''

Kristine folded her arms, and her face got a closed-in look. ''Let's talk about you for a change. Is your life so fantastic that you don't want to change it—you don't want to escape?''

''My life,'' said Danni, ''is perfectly fine.''

''Oh, right. You have a job you hate. The only reason you keep it is because Mom and Dad are thrilled one of their daughters is finally a corporate success. And then there's your love life. Basically, you don't have one.''

Now Danni stared out at the restless ocean waves. ''I date,'' she said.

''Ha. You never get beyond the first date with anyone. You haven't had anything serious since Peter. And, by the way…let's not forget you stole Peter from *me*.''

Danni shook her head. "You know it wasn't like that. Why do you keep saying it?"

Kristine, stubborn as ever, didn't answer. Danni thought back to four years ago, when her sister had been seeing Peter Mackland. But then Ted had come along, Kristine had fallen madly in love and eloped with him...and afterward Peter had turned to Danni. At first she'd offered him friendship, nothing more. It wasn't long, however, before she'd convinced herself that she was in love with him.

"What if," Kristine continued finally, as if Danni hadn't spoken. "What if you hadn't snatched Peter away from me? *You* were always the one he preferred. I could see it. But maybe...maybe if I'd felt that he truly loved me...I wouldn't have been so susceptible to Ted...."

"Oh, Kris, stop," Danni said in exasperation. "You always distort the truth. You dumped Peter, remember? I was just the consolation prize. Besides, he turned out to be an ass. You got Ted—definitely the better end of the bargain."

"I married Ted," Kristine said in a clipped tone. "That was my first mistake."

The two of them had once seemed so in love, lost in their own special world. What could have happened to bring the bitterness to Kristine's voice, the heartache to her eyes? Danni wondered.

"Don't ask," Kristine muttered. "Just don't."

It wasn't the first time Kristine had read Danni's thoughts. They were twins. They were close…no changing that, it seemed.

"Look," Danni said. "You have a habit of running away from your problems. And this time—this time you've really done it, Kris. If I weren't so damn furious at you—"

"It's not like *you* want Bryan McKay," her sister interrupted. "Or then again…maybe you do, and you just don't know how to show it."

"What I feel or don't feel about Bryan has nothing to do with it." Danni was making a supreme effort to stay calm and in control. "You've done something very wrong, Kris, and you've got to stop."

Kristine swiveled away from her. "Don't you think I know that? But I need something. I need the way Bryan makes me feel—"

"No. What you need is to work things out with Ted. *After* you've told Bryan the truth."

"All I want is a few more days," Kristine

said in a low voice. "Only a few. You can't deny me that much. After Peter...you owe me."

Danni battled a growing frustration. "No way," she said. "Forget it. You refuse to see things the way they really are, Kris. You spin fantasies, you cling to half truths—"

Kristine turned back and gave her a hard look. "If you're so against *deception,* why didn't you tell Bryan the truth yourself?"

At first Danni simply couldn't answer. She stared out at the moonlit night, remembering this afternoon...remembering the way Bryan McKay had taken her into his arms and kissed her. Just thinking about it, her skin tingled with warmth.

"He is rather hard to resist, isn't he?" Kristine remarked.

"That has nothing to do with it."

"Sure," Kristine said. "Nothing."

Danni curled her fingers against her palms. Why *hadn't* she told Bryan the truth, once she'd realized what her sister had done? Instead she'd pulled away from him, mumbled some incoherent excuse, and rushed out the door. It had all been so embarrassing and undignified. Why couldn't she have handled the matter with some authority?

Maybe her sister was right. Maybe she hadn't

told Bryan the truth because she *did* find him attractive...very attractive. But slowly another answer came to her. Perhaps deep down she'd known it all along. The main reason she hadn't enlightened Bryan was because, quite frankly, she'd felt an odd, surprisingly intense disappointment. If a man was going to kiss her the way *he'd* done, she wished that he could have told her apart from her sister. Kristine and Danni *were* different. And for once, just once, Danni wanted a man to see without being told.

"What I find most interesting of all," Kristine said astutely, "is that during your little social tête-á-tête you neglected to tell Bryan you even have a twin."

"We were just casual acquaintances. The subject of *twins* never came up. But he needs to know the truth now," Danni said. "All of it. And if you can't tell him, I certainly will—"

"No," Kristine said urgently. "Just give me a few days. I promise I'll tell Bryan—but just let me do it in my own way, my own time."

Danni pressed her hand to the window. Waves glided across the sand, surged and fell back.

"Just two days, Danni. That's all I'm asking."

Maybe, deep down, Danni was a coward. Because she certainly didn't want to be the one to tell Bryan he'd been tricked. She didn't want to see the look on his face when he found out.

"Two days, Kris," she said at last. "You have forty-eight hours...and not a minute more."

BRYAN HAD EXPECTED his mother to be taking it real easy. That had been the first thing he'd suggested. It had all happened so quickly. Son gets the midnight call. Son drops everything, flies out to Saint Louis to arrange things. Son transports mother, mother's belongings and mother's three cats back to San Diego. Thus son fulfills his dying mother's plea to live out the last few remaining months of her life in the city of her birth. So what the hell was the old gal doing perched on a high stool, dusting the pantry cabinets?

"I've hired a service, Mom. Cleaning's donc three times a week. Meals are Monday through Friday. The weekends we'll have to fend for ourselves, but that shouldn't be a problem—"

"I'm not dead yet, Bryan," his mother said, still chasing phantom cobwebs and imagined dust bunnies with a damp cloth. "I've cooked and cleaned and looked after myself since I was ten years old. That's fifty-seven years of managing things—''

''59 years, Mom. You were sixty-nine last May.''

''I know when my own birthday is,'' she muttered. She strained to reach a far corner of the pantry shelves, teetering dangerously on the edge of the stool. Bryan stepped forward, ready to stop her from toppling off. She scowled at him.

''I'm fine,'' she said. ''Just fine.''

She was anything but fine. She'd lost too damn much weight, seeming to shrink right before his eyes. Her once-thick hair hung listlessly, and new lines had etched into her face. The cancer seemed to be whittling away at her. He'd talked to the doctors in Saint Louis, rounded up the best he could find here in San Diego. They all used the same words, the same phrases. *Incurable. Inoperable. We'll make her as comfortable as we can.*

Bryan wasn't ready to give in just yet. And neither, it seemed, was his mother. She swiped her cloth along another shelf.

''You found me a very nice apartment, Bryan, even if the neighborhood is a bit upscale for my taste.''

The remark was typical of her—paying him a compliment but being sure to throw in a little criticism at the same time. Ever since he was a kid, his mother had operated on the ''don't let your son get a swelled head'' theory of parenthood. Namely, she'd done everything in her power to ensure that Bryan didn't turn out like his father: conceited and cocksure, self-important and self-indulgent.

Not that Bryan had ever had much of a chance to imitate his father. He'd only been seven when Randall McKay was killed in a boating accident. In all the years afterward, his mother had freely elaborated on her dead husband's faults. She'd dwelled on his inconsistencies, his many annoying habits...never quite able to hide how much she'd loved him in spite of his flaws or how angry she was at him for leaving her. Her complaints about him were her way of keeping him alive. Bryan had long since figured that out.

Funny thing was, lately she hadn't talked much at all about him. That worried Bryan. Of course, everything about his mother worried him these days.

''I'm not sure an apartment was the right way to go,'' he said now.

''I know you wanted to stick me in a nursing

home, Bryan. Or, even worse, have me live with you. A parent should *never* live with a grown child. It's not good for either of them."

Elizabeth McKay had a lot of rules. She was not a woman who tolerated shades of gray; she cherished absolutes.

"Okay," Bryan said, "so you won't move in with me. But what I really had in mind wasn't actually a nursing home. More of a...cooperative living arrangement, with nurses on duty—"

"Nursing home," said his mother flatly. "Doesn't matter what you call it, or how fancy it is."

Another of Elizabeth's absolutes: she would not end up in a nursing home, no matter what the circumstances. So Bryan was playing it her way, trying to give her the dignity of spending her last few months as she wished.

He felt a heaviness inside. His mother had raised him single-handedly, with virtually no help from anyone. Among his father's failings had been improvidence. Randall McKay had left his widow with no insurance, no assets and a pile of bills. After his death, she'd struggled along on a secretary's salary. And—unknown to Bryan at first—she'd cleaned houses in her off hours in order to afford a few luxuries for him. Basketball shoes, a guitar when he went through his music phase, even sailing lessons "so you'll learn not to kill yourself on the water like your poor reckless father."

Bryan still remembered the jolt he'd had at the age of twelve when, emerging from youthful self-absorption, he'd finally figured out what his mother was doing. Her long hours weren't all spent at the office typing reports and financial statements. Instead, she spent a good portion of her time mopping other people's floors, scrubbing their kitchen sinks, scouring their bathroom tiles. Pride had kept her from telling Bryan. Pride…and not wanting him to feel guilty. The day he'd learned the truth had been the beginning of manhood for him. It had given him a hearty dislike for deception, and it had made him vow someday he'd be rich enough so that his mother wouldn't have to work at all.

Of course, he hadn't counted on her stubbornness, or her independence. She'd kept right on working, well past the time when he could have supported her several times over. It had been something of a coup when at last he'd convinced her to retire. She'd chosen Saint Louis, to be near one of her girlhood friends. But now…now she was back in San Diego, trying to arrange the end of her life as neatly as she was arranging the cans on her pantry shelves.

Having set down her cloth, she'd lined up the potato soup next to the cream of tomato. "It would be nice," she said, "if you could meet someone, Bryan. Someone besides those dreadful businesswomen you usually surround yourself with."

Another backhanded compliment. "Actually," Bryan said, surprising himself, "I have met someone."

His mother perked right up. "Oh—who is she?"

He smiled a little. "You could say she's a carpenter."

Elizabeth shrugged. "That's different, at least. About time you got away from those icy corporate types."

Bryan had to smile again at that. Danni was indeed a "corporate type," but hardly icy. Maybe she'd been standoffish at first, but at their last few meetings all that had changed.

"What's her name?" Elizabeth asked.

"Danni. Danni Ferris."

"Go on," his mother said impatiently. "Is it serious?"

There was only so much he was willing to share. He didn't tell his mother a whole lot about his personal life; that was one of *his* rules.

"Bryan," said his mother, "don't keep me in suspense. Is it serious?"

Maybe there was no point in hiding the truth. Especially since his mother was so ill. And so he gave a grudging nod.

"Could be," he said. Finally, Bryan saw a smile ease the pain and weariness on his mother's face.

CHAPTER TWO

IT WAS GOING TO BE a long night at the offices of Nolan, Williams and Beck. A new account had just been dumped on Danni's desk, deadline yesterday, and she was brainstorming with the two members of her team. At least, she was attempting to brainstorm while one half of her team sat slumped over a notepad, making nonsensical doodles, and the other half rambled on.

"Mr. Nolan told me *personally* this was a very important assignment," said twenty-one-year-old Michelle in a reverent tone. Michelle was discoursing at length on her favorite subject: Mr. Nolan, chief partner in Nolan, Williams and Beck.

Larry, still doodling on his notepad, conveyed an air of world-weary cynicism. It didn't fool Danni, though. She knew all about his long-term crush on Michelle. The wonder was that Michelle didn't know.

"Mr. Nolan," said Michelle, "is putting his

full trust in us to do a first-rate job. That's exactly what he told me. His full trust.''

Larry rolled his eyes. Michelle gave him a suspicious glance.

''Mr. Nolan,'' she said, a bit more forcefully, ''is the type of person who *expects* a person to rise to the occasion. I won't let him down. He's counting on me.''

Larry rolled his eyes even more expressively this time. He didn't need to say anything, but Danni knew what he was thinking. It was the same thing *she* was thinking: the very rich and powerful, very good-looking Mr. Nolan probably didn't even know Michelle's name.

''Speaking of the job,'' Danni said, ''let's get going. We need to come up with ideas fast.'' She rubbed the crick in her neck, and frowned at the file on Hobbyhorse Toys. The company was a regional business, brand-new, rushing to launch its grand opening in time for Christmas. Apparently there had been ''creative differences'' with the previous advertising firm, and Danni was pinch-hitting late in the game. Make that *very* late. She needed some major inspiration.

A familiar tension coiled through her body. This was the nature of the business—always struggling for that one perfect idea that would excite the client and sell the product. After so many years, she ought to be used to the process by now...the endless late nights, the gallons of coffee, the deadlines threatening, the panic—followed by elation when the idea came. And then the whole cycle beginning again with another client.

Danni pulled a blank sheet of paper toward her and started doodling herself. *Think,* she commanded. *What's the angle on this one? What's going to save us this time?* She scarcely paid attention to what she was drawing until Michelle leaned over to peer.

"Designing a dream house?" she asked with interest.

Danni stared at her rough sketch. A porch with arches, a garden gate, a trellised passageway...it looked very much like Bryan McKay's house. Danni crumpled the sheet and lobbed it toward the trash can on the opposite side of the room. She kept it over there on purpose so she could practice her set shot. This time she missed. The crumpled sheet of paper landed at the feet of someone who had just appeared in the doorway—Bryan McKay. He picked it up and took his own aim. It landed neatly in the trash. Then he regarded Danni, his expression impassive.

Her heart pounded uncomfortably. She could think of only one reason he would be here. Kristine no doubt had spoken to him...and now he probably wanted Danni's explanation as well.

"Larry," she said. "Michelle. You can take a break."

The two trooped out the door. Michelle, as she went, gave Bryan an interested glance—her devotion to Mr. Nolan notwithstanding. Of course, what woman could *avoid* looking at Bryan? Tonight he wore a charcoal suit of understated sophistication, his tie loosened just a bit. With his dark eyes and darker hair, he was far too handsome for anyone's good.

When they were alone, Danni nodded toward the door. "You might as well close it," she said. "And then we'll get this over with."

He gave her a quizzical glance. "It's going to be that unpleasant?"

"After what Kris told you," she muttered, "it's bound to be."

"Who's Kris?"

She sank back in her chair. So he didn't know...Kristine hadn't talked to him yet. Danni felt the oddest mixture of despair and relief. The forty-eight hours she'd given her sister were only half over.

"Bryan, why are you here?" she asked, trying to sound as businesslike as possible.

He closed the door after all. Then he came to her desk and drew her up beside him. He put his arms around her and traced his lips across her cheek.

Unfair…so unfair. To have a man touch her like this, hold her like this, and to know it was all a mistake. She felt herself tremble.

"Danni, what's wrong?" he murmured against her ear.

She closed her eyes briefly. Then she lifted her head and gazed full at him. *See me,* she commanded silently. *See who I am.*

But he didn't see. He just brought her close once more and kissed her.

It was a very long moment before she pulled shakily away from him. She'd never known a kiss like that, not even in her dreams. Tender, sensual…possessive. Claiming her, even when he didn't know who she was.

Danni retreated to the other side of her desk. "We can't do this," she said.

"Why not?" he asked in a reasonable tone.

She folded her arms against her body, and

gazed at him as steadily as possible. "By tomorrow night you'll know the answer. I'd tell you myself, but...well, I made a promise. And I always do keep my promises."

He gave her a long, considering look. "What gives, Danni?"

"I told you—you'll find out soon enough. Twenty-four hours from now...it will all be too painfully clear."

Bryan seemed about to argue, but then seemed to think better of it. He changed tack. "So we'll talk about my house," he said.

Danni took a deep breath. "I'm sorry, Bryan, but I can't do the remodeling for you." She waved at the papers and folders strewn across her desk. "As you can see, my schedule is already overextended." She was telling the truth. Her advertising job didn't exactly leave a lot of time to spare. She had no business considering moonlighting as a carpenter. Much as she loved the idea.

"Yesterday you couldn't wait to get to work on the place," Bryan said. "I saw it in your eyes. So why are you backing off now?"

Danni gave what she hoped was a nonchalant shrug. "I can't deny it's a wonderful house. But you know that—you bought it."

His face tightened. ''I didn't buy the place for its charm.''

Danni knew she was stalling for time, but she would probably never see him again after today. Could a few more moments really matter?

''Why did you buy the house, Bryan?'' she asked.

He got a brooding look. ''Let's just say it was...a promise I made to myself. A promise fulfilled.''

It occurred to Danni that she wasn't the only one with a secret at the moment. ''Come to think of it,'' she said, ''I didn't see much furniture around. No boxes to be unpacked...I thought you'd moved in. Unless you intend to wait until after the remodeling.''

He made an impatient gesture. ''I'm not moving in. I bought the place as a sort of...investment.''

''If it *were* my house,'' Danni said, ''I'd move right in. I'd let the remodeling happen all around me. I know that would drive a lot of people crazy, but *I'd* want to be right in the thick of it, figuring out what the house needs as things go along.''

''I don't exactly want to get personal with the place,'' Bryan said dryly.

''You almost sound as if you don't like the house.''

''Let's just say it brings back memories,'' Bryan said, almost as if to himself.

Danni was more puzzled than ever, but she knew she'd delayed long enough.

''Thanks for stopping by and all,'' she said, ''but I really do have to get back to work.''

''Let's see. You ran out on me yesterday—and now you're showing me the door.''

''That's the basic idea,'' she said. ''Goodbye, Bryan.''

His eyebrows drew together. ''You act like you're not just refusing my house, you're refusing...me.''

Suddenly Danni felt impatient to have it over with. ''I don't really see that we have much of a relationship,'' she said coolly.

''That's not what you told me a few days ago. You told me you thought this could be serious.'' Bryan gazed at her so intently that she had to glance away.

Kristine. What else had Danni's sister told Bryan? Told him while pretending to be Danni?

''You can't run out on me now,'' he said softly. ''I've been advised to try something new in my life. No more corporate-type women. In fact...I've been told it's good for me to be dating a carpenter."

"Well, I *am* a corporate woman, aren't I?" Her only claim to actual carpentry experience were those long-ago summers when she'd been in her teens, and she'd helped Grandpa Daniel build his house. The summers when she'd been truly, uncomplicatedly happy.

Bryan glanced around her office, then brought his gaze back to her. "I like you better in a tool belt."

If she listened to him another second, she'd be lost. She'd find herself right back in his arms....

"Bryan, there's so much you don't know about me."

"I'm listening."

She shook her head. "It doesn't matter. You'll find out soon enough. Right now there's nothing more to say except goodbye." Quickly she went to the door and opened it. Bryan gave her another long, thoughtful glance. And then he left.

Yes, it was going to be a long night.

KRISTINE WAS FLOORING IT—and Danni hung on as the golf cart went thumping up a rise of the

Sugar Beach Country Club. As it reached the crest, the view was admittedly magnificent—the green sweep of the golf course merging into white-gold sand, the Pacific shimmering pure blue to the horizon. But then the cart went charging downward again, and Danni berated her sister.

"Stop. Enough already. You've made your point."

"And what point would that be?" Kristine asked, paying no attention to the golf clubs rattling in the back.

"That you're nothing at all like the other society wives at Sugar Beach. You don't play it safe. *You* live dangerously."

Kristine stopped the cart so abruptly that Danni almost tumbled out the front. Kristine just sat there, hands clenched in her lap, staring at the ocean. Her oversize sunglasses made it impossible to read her expression.

"Kris," Danni said at last, breaking the unnatural silence. "You haven't answered my first question yet."

"I don't know what you mean."

"You know exactly what I mean. When do you plan to tell Bryan the truth?"

Kristine went on staring straight ahead. "You

said you'd give me two days. My time's not up yet—"

"It's four o'clock in the afternoon. Your time's running out fast. And after the things he said last night—I want to make damn sure he learns the truth as soon as possible."

Now Kristine turned to look at Danni, her mouth narrowing. "You saw Bryan last night?" she asked a moment later.

"He showed up at my office. Said he thought things were getting serious between us."

"Just how *serious* did things get last night?" Kristine asked in a tight voice.

"I wish you'd listen to yourself," Danni burst out in exasperation. "You try to have an affair, pretending to be me, and then you act jealous because...I can't even go on. It's too ridiculous, and too awful at the same time."

"Just say it. *I'm* awful." Kristine was suddenly all motion. She clambered out of the cart, grabbed a golf club seemingly at random, and started off across the fairway. Danni had to hurry to catch up to her.

"Kris—"

"I don't blame you for hating me. Sometimes I hate myself. But I got so crazy when Ted...when Ted..." She couldn't seem to finish.

Instead she found her golf ball and took a forceful whack at it.

"If Ted's the problem," Danni said, "Bryan McKay isn't the solution."

Kristine marched away again, club in hand. She was wearing a very fashionable ensemble—cream-colored slacks, matching cashmere sweater, perfectly coordinated spiked shoes. You didn't live in exclusive Sugar Beach, just north of San Diego, without exhibiting the proper fashion sense. The town wasn't quite Beverly Hills in status, but it was close enough. Danni didn't much care for the Sugar Beach crowd, herself. She suspected her sister didn't either, but that was something else Kristine wouldn't confess.

Now Danni trailed after her sister. "Okay, so you won't talk about your husband. Just let me know when you plan to talk to Bryan."

"I already arranged to see him, all right?"

"Make sure you tell him everything—"

"I'm fulfilling my part of the bargain. So why are you hounding me, Danni?"

"I want..." Danni struggled with frustration. "I want to put this whole mess behind me. The mess *you* made, by the way."

Kristine stared at her from behind the protective barrier of her sunglasses. "I wish I could go back in time," she said in a low voice. "All the way back to Peter. If I'd stayed with him—if *you* hadn't ended up with him instead—everything would be different. Everything would be better."

Danni told herself to remain rational and objective. "Kris, why are you bringing up old history again? After you met Ted, you told me how glad you were that you *hadn't* ended up with Peter...that you'd broken off with him before it was too late."

Kristine went back to the cart, climbed in and sped off before Danni could catch up. Then she chugged along at a most annoying pace—just fast enough that Danni had to jog in pursuit. At last Kristine glanced over her shoulder at Danni.

"I'll tell you why I'm bringing up old stories. I think there's a pattern here. I think whenever I find a man who could actually mean something to me, you decide he has to be yours. Call it sibling rivalry, call it whatever you want—but I'm surprised you never went after Ted. Or maybe you did, behind my back."

"Kris!" Danni exclaimed, stung—and furious. She stood still. Kristine bounced along in the cart for another few yards, but then circled back. Danni glared at her. ''How could you even imagine something like that? You know me, and you *ought* to know how much I care about you. That's why I'm going to forget you ever said that. You're terribly unhappy, and you're taking it out on me.''

Kristine maintained her bravado for another few seconds, but then her face crumpled. She took off the sunglasses, and Danni saw her reddened eyes. She looked as if she'd been crying for hours.

''Oh, Kris—''

''Danni, if you ask me what's wrong, I swear I'll hit you with a three wood.'' Tears spilled down Kristine's cheeks, and she swiped at them. ''I can't have anyone here see me like this,'' she mumbled. ''You don't know what they're like, Danni. They're always watching, waiting for one little misstep, one little show of vulnerability they can use against me. And all the while they're pretending to be my devoted friends. I never feel *safe* anymore.''

''So much for high society. Come on,'' Danni said, climbing into the cart beside her sister. ''Put the sunglasses on, and no one will be able to tell.''

Kristine replaced the protective barrier, but

her mouth had a pinched look. ''I'm sorry for what I said, Danni. You're the only real friend I *do* have left.''

Danni sighed. ''That doesn't change the fact that I'm ticked at you, big time. It's bad enough that you pretended to be me. But letting Bryan believe things could be serious—''

''All right, all right, I know it's impossible.'' Now Kristine sounded miserable again. ''I don't want to hurt Bryan.'' And then, in a low voice, she added, ''There's been enough hurting already.''

''Kristine—''

''No more questions, Danni. I told you I'd come clean with Bryan, and I will. Tonight, in my own way.'' The cart took off again at a good clip. Kristine gripped the wheel, staring straight ahead, and Danni no longer had the heart to chastise her. Besides, she had a niggling feeling inside, a fear that there might be a grain of truth to what Kristine had said. Was it possible that Danni *did* have some destructive need to compete with her sister when it came to men? And, if it was true, how could she ever have a sound relationship with a man...an enduring relationship...

"Oh, no," Kristine said. "It's *him.* He's coming right toward us."

For a wild moment, Danni thought Kristine was talking about Bryan McKay. But no... Bryan wasn't in the golf cart approaching them. Instead her sister's husband was at the wheel.

Kristine floored their own cart all over again—speeding away from Ted.

"Kris, this is ridiculous," Danni said, hanging on for dear life. "At least, think of what your Sugar Beach friends will have to say about *this.*"

After a moment, the cart came to a jolting stop. Ted rode up beside them.

"Hello, Danni," he said. And then, after an awkward pause, "Hello, Kris."

At forty-one, Ted was still an extremely handsome man—tall, well-constructed, solidly built. Even if he *was* starting to gray a bit around the edges, settle a bit, the look suited him. However, right now his face was strained in a way Danni had never seen before.

"Kris, I don't know what the hell you think you're doing," he told his wife. "But you've got to stop."

"I asked you to leave me alone." Kristine's

voice wobbled. "Can't you do that much for me?"

"No. Why should I? You're mad at me, but you don't even know what's going on. You won't even listen—"

"I don't want to hear! Can't you understand? That will only make it worse. Listening to all the reasons. The explanations, the excuses..."

"No excuses," Ted muttered. "When you're ready to hear me out, you let me know. When you're ready to stop thinking about yourself, you let me know. I'll be waiting...for a little while."

"A little while?" Kristine's voice was clogged with tears. She and her husband stared at each other, locked in their own private torment. Danni felt like an intruder, but there was nowhere to retreat. The golf course spread out all around them in its lovely emerald green...offering no reprieve anywhere. Nonetheless, she started to climb out of the cart. Kristine reached out a hand to her.

"No, Danni—please," she implored. "Don't leave me."

Ted looked from one sister to the other. "Oh, hell," he said heavily. Then he turned his cart around, and drove back the way he had come. Kristine waited until he had left before she broke down. Danni put an arm around her sister, and tried to comfort her.

The twin who infuriated her…the twin whom she loved.

CHAPTER THREE

THE THRILL of the hunt. That was the main thing Bryan liked about his work. It was his job to put money and people together for big projects, big dreams. In the process, he got called a lot of different names: venture capitalist, risk taker. Gambler. Damn fool, even, according to one client, until the client's investment came back twentyfold.

And now Bryan was on the hunt for new game. It had taken him over three weeks to set up this appointment with the evasive C. J. Whitfield. At last the man had agreed to meet Bryan in this small restaurant in the heart of San Diego's Old Town.

Bryan ordered a beer, sat back and listened to the haunting flute playing somewhere outside in the cool air. It was music that put him in mind of Danni Ferris. Of course, just about everything put him in mind of Danni lately. He was still thinking about her when someone slipped into the chair across the table.

"Mr. McKay." It was a statement, not a question, spoken by a slender brunette in her thirties. She gazed at him appraisingly, almost challengingly. It only took him a second or two to figure out who she was.

"The C.J. is misleading," he said.

She ordered a cappuccino. "For some reason, people just assume C.J. is going to belong to some stodgy good old boy. Beats me why they don't figure it could stand for Candace Jennifer as well as anything else."

She didn't look like either a Candace or a Jennifer. She looked like...a C.J. Someone who enjoyed hiding behind an air of mystery and then taking others by surprise. Bryan wasn't impressed. He considered all the delays he'd gone through to get this appointment—the cancellations, the rearrangements. It was too elaborate. Too devious, in the end.

"Well, Mr. McKay. Start convincing me why I should do business with you and your friends."

Bryan tried to remind himself that this was the part he liked, working to match the money with the dream. And it was a very good dream this time, belonging to a group of local architects and artists who wanted to revitalize a section of the San Diego-Tijuana border zone. An ambitious building project was in the offing—an innovative cluster of apartment buildings, a commercial district, an artisans' compound. Bryan explained it all to C. J. Whitfield over broiled bass and asparagus soup. The soup was a mistake. And so, too, it seemed, was C.J.

"Tell me, Bryan. Why did you come to me on this one?"

"You have a reputation for imaginative thinking."

"I also have a reputation for being filthy rich," she remarked.

"That, too," he said easily.

She almost smiled. "Funny thing is, Bryan McKay, *you* have a reputation for picking winners. But this time...I just don't see it. For one thing, it's a lousy location. Nobody wants to go anywhere near that part of town anymore. Nothing you build there is going to change that."

"This group is going to change a lot of things," he argued. "They have a certain vision—"

"Oh, no. When people start getting visionary, it always means trouble. Bryan, I'm as idealistic as the next poor schmuck, but I also believe in confronting reality. From what I've heard, so do you. Why this fanciful turn of yours?''

She was getting on his nerves, but he didn't actually have a good answer for her. This wasn't the first time he'd gambled on an idea that seemed impractical or even impossible at first. But there was something special about this project, something that captured his excitement in a way few other ideas had.

C.J. thumbed through the prospectus he'd handed her. ''Sure, all the figures look fine on paper,'' she said disparagingly.

Bryan found himself comparing her to Danni, and couldn't imagine two women more different from each other. Maybe Danni was elusive in her own way, but she was also completely...genuine. Bryan liked the sound of that word. It suited Danni. He couldn't imagine her deliberately creating an aura of mystery, couldn't picture her staging an entrance or an exit for effect. Which was what C.J. was doing at the moment—staging her exit. She flicked her hand in the air, and a younger woman who had remained unobtrusive until now materialized to stand a respectful distance away. Bryan wouldn't have been surprised if she'd curtseyed to her boss.

C.J. tossed the prospectus toward her assistant; the woman turned out to be a good catch.

"I'll look the figures over again as a personal favor. But I wouldn't get my hopes up, Bryan, if I were you."

"Message received," he said. "I won't hold my breath waiting for your call."

She treated him to another of her challenging looks. "Oh, I *will* call you," she said. Was she actually *flirting* with him? Then she rose from her chair and swirled out of the restaurant, assistant in her wake.

Bryan finished his beer, paid the tab and wandered outside. Old Town was best at night like this, the ancient adobe buildings mellow in the golden spill of lanterns. He paused at the tiled fountain in the plaza where passersby tossed their coins for wishes and good luck. The flute music still played from somewhere just out of sight...wistful, restless. Reminding Bryan of Danni Ferris all over again.

When he let himself into his apartment a short time later, the phone was ringing. He picked it up, said hello, and heard her voice. It was oddly subdued.

"Hello, Bryan. I...can't make it tonight, after all. I'm sorry."

''What gives, Danni?'' He seemed to say that to her a lot.

There was a long pause on the other end of the line. And then, all in a rush she continued, ''I was supposed to tell you something tonight. But I chickened out. I know that as soon as I tell you...you'll despise me. And I don't think I can bear it.''

She had a habit of speaking in riddles. ''Come over,'' he said. ''We'll talk it out. Nothing can be as bad as you make it sound.''

She was quiet at that, so quiet he almost thought he'd lost the connection.

''Danni,'' he asked, ''still there?''

''Yes,'' she said, her voice low. She paused again. ''Bryan what made you show up at my office last night?''

''I wanted to see you.''

''And when you saw me,'' she continued, ''didn't anything seem strange to you? Didn't anything seem *different?*''

He couldn't figure out where she was headed. ''You seemed,'' he said honestly, ''more beautiful than ever.''

If he thought he was going to flatter her, he was wrong. The silence on the other end of the line was now potent.

"Danni—"

"Goodbye, Bryan. I can't see you anymore." She hung up abruptly, without another word.

He gazed thoughtfully at the phone and then he, too, hung up. "What the hell was that all about?" he muttered.

DANNI FOUND HER SISTER kneeling in the garden, digging up bulbs. Kristine wielded her spade with rather more force than necessary, the rich dark earth building up around her and the poor bulbs tossed aside unceremoniously.

"Didn't you and Ted plant those together?" Danni asked. "The first year you were married."

Kristine pushed aside a strand of hair, leaving a dirt smudge on her face. "I'm sick of these damn tulips," she muttered.

"Kris, you always loved those flowers."

"It's time for a change." Another bulb went flying. "Why, it's almost Thanksgiving. And then Christmas…and then a brand-new year. A perfect time to completely overhaul my life."

Danni knelt beside her sister. "Kris—talk to me."

Kristine ducked her head, the blond hair falling forward again to obscure her face. "No doubt you want to know every little fact about last night. You want to know all about how I confessed to Bryan, and what he said in return, and…and every humiliating detail.''

Danni regarded her sister. ''I would like to know that it's taken care of at last.''

Kristine didn't even seem to be listening. ''Can you imagine what it's like, Danni? To have a husband who no longer wants you.''

''From what I saw yesterday on the golf course,'' she said, ''you and Ted may still have a lot to work out. But he still cares about you a great deal. No one could get that angry, and not care.''

''You don't know, Danni. You don't know what a man can do to make you feel…completely undesirable. Completely unwanted. After that, there's not much he can do to convince you otherwise.''

''Kris, what happened? What did Ted do to make you feel this way?''

''I can't talk about it,'' Kristine said, gripping her spade. ''I just can't. I can't say it out loud…don't ask me to, Danni.''

Danni had never seen her sister like this. Kristine had been many things in her life—impetuous, thoughtless, self-centered…extravagantly penitent when she realized she'd strained the limits of a friendship. But she had never been this way—so despairing, and so unsure of herself.

"Kris, if you'd only talk to me," Danni said gently. "Maybe I can help—"

The spade was digging again. "Don't even try, Danni. All you really want to know right now is what happened with Bryan. Well...I'll tell you." She sounded defiant, her words recklessly gathering speed. "I went to meet Bryan last night, and I told him the whole sorry situation. I told him how I'd pretended to be you, and how you hadn't known anything about it until it was too late. I asked him not to blame *you* at least. But he wouldn't listen. He told me...he told me he was disgusted with both of us, and he never wanted to see either one of us again!"

DANNI JUST KNEW it was going to be a lousy Thanksgiving. Of course, that was a safe bet—Thanksgiving at her parents' house always turned out to be a dismal failure. Every year her mother and father tried a different combination of guests. And every year the result was the same: discreet yawns, embarrassed excuses for leaving early. Of course, Jay and Leah Ferris would never admit that their get-togethers were…well, boring.

Now Danni stood on her parents' front porch, balancing her usual offerings of sweet-potato casserole and mushroom-sage stuffing. Her mother swung open the door and gave her a hug that almost upended the sweet potatoes. If nothing else, Danni could count on an enthusiastic greeting. She knew she was the success story of the family, the one who had fulfilled all her parents' expectations. They didn't even mind that she was thirty and still unmarried. Plenty of time for that later, they always told her. Solidify your career before slowing yourself down with a family.

Leah ushered Danni inside. "Thank goodness you're finally here. When I found out Kristine and Ted couldn't make it—"

"Kristine isn't here?"

"Darling, that's what I'm trying to tell you. Apparently they've had some sort of…altercation. Ted flew out to be with his family in Sacramento, and Kristine simply refused to say where *she'd* be."

Danni felt a letdown. No matter how angry she got at her sister, she always counted on Kristine to be at family functions. It was the one thing that made these occasions bearable.

Now Danni went with her mother to the kitchen, and set down both casserole dishes.

"Are you all right?" her mother asked with a worried frown. "You don't seem very chipper."

At times her mother could be quite observant although her quaint terms often irritated Danni. This time, however, Danni had to admit she did *not* feel chipper. Ever since those few days ago, when she'd learned that Bryan never wanted to see her again...it had put a damper on her enthusiasm. Regret and sadness would wash over her at the most inconvenient times.

"I'm fine, Mom," she said with an effort.

"Everything going okay at work?"

Danni had a wild urge to lie—to say that she'd walked out on her advertising job and that she'd decided to become a full-time carpenter. She didn't say anything, though. She just busied herself at the sink, rinsing the lettuce for the salad. Her mother gave her a sharp look, but then hurried out to the living room to try entertaining her guests.

Two hours later, it was painfully clear that the guests refused to be entertained. Danni glanced around the dining room table. She sat among a few of her mother's law partners, several more of her father's management associates, two of the neighbors from down the street. It was not a congenial group. Conversations proceeded in fits and starts, then faded to nonexistence. The turkey was dry, the cranberry sauce tart, the pumpkin pie bland. Danni saw the look of chagrin on her mother's face, but also knew that she would refuse to give up. Leah was no doubt already calculating a brand-new guest list for Christmas.

Danni picked at her mincemeat pie, only to set down her fork at last. She saw the elderly man on her left give a rather desperate peek at his watch. She knew she should be trying to liven the party; she owed her parents that much. But all she could think about was Bryan. She tried to remind herself that they'd only been casual acquaintances until Kristine had stepped in and distorted everything. But the sense of loss continued to assault her.

Fool, a voice mocked in her head. *Maybe it's true. Maybe you only care about men your sister wants.*

She clenched her hands in her lap. She didn't want to care about Bryan McKay. She scarcely knew him.

"Danni, are you sure you're all right?" Leah asked. "You've hardly touched your food."

"Yes...I'm fine."

"She works too hard," Leah confided to someone across the table. There was a note of pride in her voice. Leah herself had worked hard all her life, the first one in her family to get a college degree. No wonder she took her career so seriously, and expected Danni to do the same. If only Danni's career *could* provide all the answers...if only it could make her stop thinking about a man she couldn't have....

She stood abruptly. "Mom, Dad—I'm sorry, but I have to leave."

The gentleman to her left stole another glance at his watch. "Sorry, but I have to be on my way, too," he said. There were other relieved murmurs and rustlings around the table.

Danni knew she was responsible for breaking up the party even earlier than usual. Her mother sent her an accusing glare, and she felt guilty. But she just had to get out of here.

Somehow she had to outrun her thoughts of Bryan McKay.

IT HAD BEEN a bad day for Elizabeth. She'd insisted on trying to make Thanksgiving dinner—

only to overexert herself, and ending up huddled on the sofa with her famous cornbread dressing and her pumpkin pies only half-done. Bryan had been grateful for the nursing service he'd hired against all her protests. This afternoon, the nurse on duty had come to the rescue—finishing up the dinner, making Elizabeth as comfortable as possible. But Bryan still blamed himself. He shouldn't have let his mother do all that work. Never mind that she'd been looking forward to it for days. It was up to him to make certain she didn't overdo it.

Night had fallen, and he'd finally left his mother asleep in her apartment, the nurse still in charge. Now he climbed out of his car and went up the walk to his own apartment. A shape emerged from the darkness next to his door. Danni. He couldn't think of anyone he'd rather see. After the way she'd hung up the phone on him the other night, this was an unexpected pleasure. Before she could protest, he put his arms around her.

"You smell good," he said. His hands moved over her back.

"Bryan, I shouldn't be here," she answered. "It's a mistake. But somehow...somehow I can't help myself."

"I've missed you," he said. He unlocked the door and drew her inside. When he turned on the hall lamp, light spilled over her blond hair. Her face had an unhappy look, but he intended to do something about that. He held her close again, kissing her, and he could sense the tension begin to leave her body.

"Bryan...I've wanted this...."

"Me, too," he murmured against her throat. He was impeded by some long, silky scarf she had draped around her neck. She was all dressed up, but he liked her better when she wore jeans. Not to mention her tool belt. He went on holding her...he went on touching her.

She tensed all over again and pulled away.

"Bryan, this isn't supposed to happen. I just thought if I could see you again...if only for a moment...if I could *ask* you..."

Clearly she was in turmoil, and Bryan tried to help her. "Ask me anything," he said.

She took a deep breath. "Bryan, do you find me...desirable?"

"You know I do."

She shook her head. "No, I don't. Not really."

"I'll show you." He brought her into his arms again. And he proceeded to show her. It was a very long while before she broke away again. Her face was flushed.

"No," she whispered. "I can't do this! It's not right."

He didn't agree. As far as he was concerned, nothing had ever seemed more right.

"I want to make love to you, Danni," he said. "I think it's time."

She took in a deep, quavering breath. "Oh, Bryan..."

It was several kisses later when he began unbuttoning her dress. Too bad they were very small buttons, and there were so many of them. Meanwhile, the scarf thing kept getting in his way.

"We have to stop," she said, placing her hands over his. "This isn't right."

"It's right," he said. "Trust me." He finally got rid of the scarf. It drifted to the floor, allowing him much better access. He kissed the places he'd managed to expose, and was rewarded with a sigh from Danni. She curled her fingers in his hair.

"Bryan, if you knew what it meant to me...to have a man want me...a man like you..."

"Yes," he said. "I want you."

Something sparked in her eyes, a flash of

spirit. "It can't really be wrong. Not when... It just can't be wrong."

She was talking in riddles again, but he figured the time for talking was past. He drew her toward the bedroom. She hesitated another second, but then she gave an almost imperceptible nod—as if she'd just won some argument with herself.

And then she came to him.

CHAPTER FOUR

IT WAS THE DAY AFTER Thanksgiving, and very early in the morning. Danni buried her head under the pillow, refusing to acknowledge the knocking at her apartment door. "Go away," she mumbled crankily.

But the knocking wouldn't stop. Whoever it was demanded an answer. Stumbling out of bed, Danni went to the door and squinted through the peephole. Bryan McKay stood on the other side.

Her pulses surged, as if responding to some magnetic force. For a crazy moment, she considered scurrying back to bed and pulling the covers up over her ears. But she knew she couldn't hide from Bryan forever. He knew the truth now. Kristine had told him about the subterfuge—how she had duped him into believing the two sisters were one—and that she'd been playing the part of her twin. If he never wanted to forgive either one of them, that was his privilege. If he wanted to berate Danni for having such an uncontrollable twin sister, that was also his privilege. Taking a deep breath, she put her hand on the door knob and began to turn it.

But then her courage failed her. She couldn't face his disillusionment right now. His disappointment...his anger. And so she did retreat to bed. She did pull the covers over her head. And she hoped with all her heart that Bryan would simply go away.

BRYAN MCKAY STOOD outside the door to Danni's apartment. He knew she was in there. He'd seen a shadow through the peephole—he'd seen the door knob start to turn. But now all was silence, no answer. Why was she hiding from him?

Okay, so perhaps he knew the answer to that. Last night, his lovemaking with Danni hadn't gone at all well. She'd been guarded, almost furtive, as if afraid to let any passion show. They'd gone through the motions together...but there'd been little pleasure between them. Afterward she'd left as quickly as possible, hardly saying a word.

So now, understandably, she was embarrassed. She didn't want to see him—didn't even want to talk to him. Somehow he had to reassure her that their lovemaking would go much better next time. And he had to convince her there should be a next time.

He knocked again...and again. He waited, knocked some more.

"Danni," he called out. "I know you're in there."

A few more knocks, and a few moments later, the door swung open at last, revealing a rumpled Danni in rumpled pajamas.

"So now you know everything," she said without ceremony. "And I'm sure you're here to tell me how disappointed you are. Believe me, I understand."

"Disappointed," he echoed. "Perhaps. I know there's a problem. But I think we can deal with it."

She stared at him distrustfully. "You're taking this much better than I thought you would. I thought you'd be so mad you'd never want to see me again."

"Mad...why would I be mad?" he asked, puzzled.

"Why *wouldn't* you be," she muttered.

Danni was taking it far too seriously. This type of thing happened—the first time you made love to someone could be awkward.

"We just need a little practice," he told her, smiling.

She frowned. "Practice...?"

Bryan searched for exactly the right words to reassure her. "A person would be a fool," he said, "to throw away an entire relationship because it got off to a rocky start. And Danni...you should know by now, I'm no fool. Despite what's happened, I believe there could be something between us. If we get to know each other better...get closer...I think we can work it out."

She didn't seem convinced. "Bryan, maybe we can talk about it, but—"

"I didn't come here to talk," he said gently. "I don't think that's the solution. We should just spend some time together."

"That's not the best idea in the world," she said. "Not after everything—"

"Just spend some time with me," he said. "We'll drive somewhere. I'll wait here while you change...although I do like you in pj's."

She drew her eyebrows together. "You make it all sound too easy. But I know you're angry, no matter what you say."

If she thought that, she really did feel bad about their lovemaking. "I don't think anything is going to be easy," he said. "But let's try to give things a fresh start, Danni. Let's give ourselves a chance, at least.''

Her look seemed to waver between hope and sadness. At last, though, she gave a reluctant nod. ''You wait...I'll change.'' The door swung shut on him—but, despite Danni's overreaction to their physical miscue, he felt a hopefulness lighten his mood.

THE RASPBERRY VEST or the tartan blouse...? Uninspired, Danni tossed both across the base of her bed and began rummaging through her closet. But then she happened to glance across at her bureau, and saw the photo there; herself and Kristine, smiling into the camera.

Danni walked over to the bureau and glared at the photograph. *He's trying to act like he's not angry anymore, Kris, but that's just not possible. After what we did to him...of course he's angry. Why did you have to pretend you were me? Why did you try to steal my life?*

The picture of her smiling sister gave away no secrets. Danni plunked it facedown, and then she started to get dressed. Yes, she would spend time with Bryan—she owed him that much.

If she was going to pay for what her sister did, she just wanted to get it over with.

"YOU REALLY are beautiful."

These were the words Bryan uttered as he and Danni walked from her apartment to the elevator. She flushed when she saw the expression in his eyes. She'd finally chosen an outfit that usually gave her confidence: a peach-colored blouse and slim jeans in biscuit brown. She'd also swept her hair into a loose chignon. Unfortunately, they were the only two people in the elevator, so Danni found herself shut in a small, intimate space with Bryan McKay.

"Strange," he said. "You're a carpenter at heart. You want to build things. So why do you live in an apartment, instead of your own house? A home you could remodel as much as you wanted."

He'd had no way of knowing that he was talking about her dreams...her own home where she could tear down walls, replace windows, put on an addition or two. But pursuing her advertising career simply hadn't left a lot of time for such indulgences.

Her gaze strayed to the Stop button. Maybe being confined to a small space with him *wasn't* such a bad idea. They could stay in here until Bryan finally said everything he needed to say. The necessary recriminations...

Bryan, it seemed, had followed the direction of her glance. "My thoughts exactly," he murmured. "We could settle in here pretty comfortably, don't you think?"

"No—that's not what I had in mind...."

He leaned her against the wall of the elevator. Every time he touched her it was like this...the warmth coursing through her, turning so quickly to need. She seemed powerless to resist. And so, with a sigh of surrender, she arched her throat so that he could trail his mouth against her skin.

The only thing that saved her was that *he* hadn't pressed the Stop button. The elevator reached the lobby, and the doors glided open. Danni pulled away from Bryan, averted her gaze from the doorman, and hurried outside. Her body still tingled from Bryan's caresses.

"I thought we were having fun," he remarked as he caught up to her.

Fun...Danni wouldn't call it that. Sweet torture, perhaps.

Bryan led her to a navy-blue sports car complete with ragtop. She recognized it as a very expensive model, all aerodynamic curves. Bryan, apparently, had his indulgences.

"Nice," Danni commented as she settled into

the passenger seat. Bryan climbed into the driver's seat and started the engine. He drove down the street, his hand easy on the gearshift knob, taking a right turn, then a left. Eventually he pulled up at a small, unassuming coffee shop not far from the harbor.

"Can't take you anywhere without breakfast," Bryan announced. "How do waffles sound? They make the best in town here."

To her surprise, Danni found that she was quite hungry. "Waffles sound wonderful," she admitted.

A short while later, she discovered that he was right. For all its unadorned atmosphere, this restaurant served possibly the best waffles she'd ever tasted.

"You like the good things in life, don't you, Bryan?" she asked, when she couldn't eat another bite. "You're...a connoisseur. Something tells me you don't take second best."

He smiled a little grimly. "Okay, I have a confession to make. I grew up poor. The kind of poor where you're just one step away from not making the rent, one step away from skipping lunch because you can't afford three meals a day. That's how it was for a long time after my dad died. So I guess I did get a taste for what I couldn't have. And when I could finally afford a few things...yeah, I knew what I wanted."

"I wasn't accusing you," she said.

"They say you never really stop being the kid you once were."

Absentmindedly she traced a pattern on the table top. "I think that's true. I think I'm still twelve years old at heart, wishing it was summer so I could be out of school and spending more time with Grandpa Daniel."

"Tell me about him," Bryan said.

"He never seemed to expect too much of me," she said slowly. "He wasn't like my parents at all. They always had very specific ideas of what they wanted from me. But not Grandpa Daniel. When I was with him...I could just *be.* And we'd build things. If I didn't know how to use a framing squarc, or if I smacked my thumb with the hammer...Grandpa just showed me how to do it right. I was always happy that my parents named me after him. Danielle for Daniel."

"When did you lose him?" Bryan asked after a moment.

"I was nineteen. He was sick for a while...too long, actually. But I didn't want him to go. I wanted to hang on. I wanted *him* to hang on. And he did, as long as he could, even though the pain was getting bad. He was eighty years old, but I think he was still a kid inside, too."

Bryan reached across the table and took her hand. "I'm sorry," he said.

Danni blinked against sudden tears. "I still miss him—you know that? It's been eleven years, but sometimes I wake up in the morning and think of something I need to tell him. Like the fact that I was down at the hardware store, and I saw the perfect sliding compound miter saw. Grandpa Daniel was the only one who'd be interested in something like that."

"Hey, I'm interested. I understand the importance of a good saw."

Danni tried to smile. "You're being nice."

"Never tell a guy he's nice. Destroys any image he ever had of himself."

So...*nice* wasn't the right word for Bryan. Danni could think of a lot of other ones. *Devastatingly handsome. Sexy. Appealing*—any way you looked at him...

She was getting on the wrong track. But when she tried to tug her hand from his, he held fast.

"Why do you keep trying to run away?"

"I'm sitting right here, aren't I?"

"Yet you want to run away," he said.

She gazed at their linked fingers. "What I really want to do is talk about what happened. About me and my sis—"

"We'll talk about it later," Bryan said easily. "Right now the day is too good to waste."

Danni tried to argue, but Bryan was in no mood to listen.

And so they were soon in the little blue sportster again, making their way to one of the docks along San Diego Bay.

"Let me guess," Danni said. "You have a boat. Not a very big one, probably. Just the nicest boat in the bay."

"It's seaworthy," he said in a gruff tone.

That turned out to be an understatement. It was a gorgeous boat—light polished wood fashioned into intriguing nooks and crannies, expert craftsmanship in every detail. After clearing the docks, Bryan hoisted the sails and they made their way into the bay. Sunlight sparkled on the water, lulling Danni into a false sense of comfort.

"Want to take the helm?" Bryan asked.

"No way," she said. "I'd probably just end up crashing this thing."

"You're a Californian, and you don't know

how to sail? We'll have to do something about that,'' he said.

After a brief tour of the bay, Bryan docked at Coronado Island. It was actually a peninsula, not an island, but Danni had always liked to think of it as a place separate and apart from the mainland...a place to dream. It had been quite some time since she'd been here, but as a kid this had been one of her favorite haunts.

It wasn't much of a walk from the boat to the Hotel del Coronado. Danni had loved this magnificent old building as a kid. It fronted the ocean in Victorian splendor, red turrets rising to beckon travelers. Danni and Bryan walked along the beach just beyond the hotel, leaving footprints in the white sand.

''Sometimes Grandpa Daniel and I came here on the weekends,'' she said finally, her memories demanding to be spoken. ''He'd take me to lunch at the hotel, and talk about ceiling beams and floor joists. And then we'd come walk on the beach...just the way you and I are doing now. No particular destination in mind. We'd wait until sunset, and then we'd drive back home over the bridge. And I would have such a sense of satisfaction...as if I knew a day couldn't possibly be more well spent.''

She bent down and poked her fingers in the wet sand, unearthing a shell. She remembered coming home those long-ago days with her pockets full of sand and shells.

Bryan knelt beside her. "Danni, you can feel that way again. A day so well spent you can't imagine it any other way."

Maybe that was true. Maybe she was building more memories right now, to keep with her.

"The funny thing is, Bryan…you remind me a little of Grandpa Daniel. Nothing I can put my finger on, exactly. Just the fact that every now and then…well, I almost relax around you."

"Almost," he repeated. "Doesn't sound like much of an endorsement."

"How *can* I relax," she burst out, "if you won't tell me what you're really feeling about me and Kris—"

"Danni." Once again he silenced her with a kiss. And once again he got that sympathetic look, as if he were dealing with some volatile creature who needed gentling. Danni didn't know whether to be exasperated, or simply to give in to the moment.

She gave in. This time she was the one who

kissed Bryan, there in the dazzling sunlight as the waves of the Pacific lapped against their feet. She kissed him, and never wanted the magic to end.

CHAPTER FIVE

KRISTINE WAS WORKING the hospital floor like a pro. She paused here and there to speak to a doctor or a nurse or a patient, then moved on gracefully. She looked every bit the stylish society wife on her charitable rounds—pristine white linen dress, the arms of her equally pristine white sweater tied jauntily around her neck. Danni wondered if she was the only one who saw the etchings of strain around Kristine's eyes and mouth.

At last Danni managed to corner her sister. "Kris, we have to talk. You can't keep avoiding me. I'm just lucky I was able to track you down here."

"Danni, so glad you could make it. Luncheon will be served in the conference room across the hall—"

"Dammit, Kris, I'm not one of your snobby friends. Stop with the act and *talk* to me."

Kristine glanced around. "Keep your voice

down,'' she muttered. ''Do you want somebody to find out I'm in the middle of a major personal crisis?''

''It might be refreshing for once if you'd just let it all hang out.''

Kristine took Danni's elbow and steered her along the hall to the nurses' lounge. She poked her head inside the room.

''All clear,'' she said, and ushered Danni inside. ''Whatever you want to say—do it now, and be quick about it. This is a very important event for me. I can't afford to have anything go wrong. I'm in *charge,* for goodness' sake.'' Kristine made it sound as if she were president of the United States, not merely chairperson of the Saint Pius Hospital Children's Fund.

''All right, I'll make this quick,'' Danni said. ''Bryan came to see me yesterday. We went to Coronado Island and...well, that's beside the point. The point is—''

''Bryan came to see you?'' Kris got a peculiar look on her face.

''Yes. He showed up at my apartment, insisting that we spend the day together. But he was just too...too damn understanding about the whole miserable mess you created.''

"Too understanding..." Kristine echoed. She sank into a chair.

"He wouldn't even let me talk about it," Danni continued. "So I'm beginning to wonder...what exactly *did* you tell him, Kris? Did you somehow make yourself out to be a saint?"

"Maybe I don't want to talk about it, either," Kristine muttered, clenching her hands on the table top before her.

"Well, *somebody* had better talk about it," Danni said grimly. "And you're elected."

Kristine ducked her head. "Why can't you just be happy, Danni? Bryan wants to spend time with you...in spite of everything. You've won."

"Dammit, Kris, this isn't a contest!" Danni sat down across from her sister and gazed at her intently. "What exactly did you tell Bryan?"

"I told him the truth," Kristine said woodenly, staring straight ahead. "I told him I'd pretended to be you a couple of times. I told him you weren't to blame at all. He seemed furious, like I said. I guess he's gotten over it. End of story."

Danni battled a supreme frustration. "Nothing can be that simple."

"Maybe it can be," Kristine said in a low voice. "Maybe people get exactly what they deserve in life. You've always been the one who does things right. I've always been the one who messes up. So why shouldn't you be the one who ends up with a man like Bryan...and I'm the one who ends up with...nothing at all!''

As usual, Kristine was being overly dramatic. But she'd never sounded quite this wretched before, and all the old sympathies came rushing back. Danni reached out and clasped her sister's hand.

''Kris, don't count Ted out yet. Whatever he's done...let him try to make it up to you.''

Kristine jumped up. She strode over to the coffee machine and poured herself a cup. Then she cradled her hands around it as if trying to warm herself.

''You don't understand, Danni.''

''So explain it to me.''

Kristine shook her head. ''No. It doesn't matter any more. All that matters is...Bryan wants to be with you. So let him, Danni. Let it be that simple.''

In her heart, Danni wanted it to be that easy. But she was a realist, too. How did that old saying go?

If something seemed too good to be true...it probably was.

"I'M GLAD YOU CAME." Bryan stood there smiling at Danni, more gorgeous and masculine than ever in jeans and polo shirt. Danni stared at him, her heart seeming to thrum in her ears. It was always like this when she saw him—her body seemed to respond with a will of its own. Right now, she was almost leaning toward him, as if the physical need to be near him could not be denied.

She took a step back, struggling for distance. He'd called, and asked her to meet him at this trolley stop. He'd refused to explain why.

"Bryan," she said, "I only came because we *do* have to talk. About—"

"No talking about that," he said. "You seem to keep tormenting yourself…refusing to believe I don't care about what happened. So…I'll just have to show you." He smiled again, and she felt as if she were melting inside.

Maybe it is this simple….

The trolley came, and soon they were traveling south on the Blue Line.

They sat side by side, Bryan holding Danni's hand tucked in his, as the city streamed past the windows.

"Where are you taking me?" Danni asked.

"You'll see," was all he'd say, maddeningly

mysterious. And so they sat in silence, every nerve ending of Danni's alive to Bryan's nearness. She was almost sorry when it came time to get off the trolley.

A car met them, driven by a pleasant burly man whom Bryan introduced as Robert Serna. "Robert's an old college buddy of mine. He's also an architect, working with me on a project," Bryan explained.

Danni got into the front seat of the sedan, Bryan climbed in back, and Robert started the engine. Danni, however, soon found herself caught up in the men's conversation. She learned that Bryan was handling the financing end of a building venture planned by Robert's architectural firm. Listening, she heard the enthusiasm in Bryan's voice. This was her first glimpse of his professional life. How little she knew about him! And yet...and yet in some ways she felt as if she had known him forever.

They came to a dingy area of town—old warehouses, abandoned buildings, narrow streets. But Bryan and Robert both behaved as if this were a place of limitless possibilities. They piled out of the car, bringing Danni with them, explaining their plans for the area: the warehouse in front of them would be restored into clean airy apartments centered around an expansive park, a shopping area bordering on the park, too, with a whole series of artisans' and artists' workshops.

"The idea," said Robert, "is to open up the space. We Californians are getting too much in the habit of closing ourselves in—gated communities and the like. There will be no gates here."

Danni glanced all around. "You'll be building something durable," she murmured. "I can feel it. If you need an extra set of hands...I'll be down here with my hammer and my framing square in a second." She stopped, feeling a little foolish, but then she caught Bryan's gaze, saw the approval in his eyes. It warmed her.

An hour sped by as they walked around the area, discussing all the details. Danni found herself on the samc wavelength as Robert, sharing ideas about design and construction. He treated her as an equal, and she liked that. Grandpa Daniel had once told her that he'd run across more than a few architects who looked down their noses at carpenters. But Robert Serna didn't behave that way at all.

"Not many architects know how to actually build something," he said. "Myself, I spent a couple of years working for a construction firm—I know my way around a chop saw.''

Danni smiled at him. He was a friend of Bryan's, and she could picture him as her friend, too.

If it really could be this easy. If I really could picture a future with Bryan.

It was late afternoon by the time Robert dropped Bryan and Danni at Bryan's house. She stood outside with him for a moment, appreciating the place. It had been fashioned in the Spanish mission style so popular in California a century ago—whitewashed walls with bull-nose corner bead, a row of arches along the porch, red tile roof. Yet Danni saw unique details, too…the garden door in the wall to the right, the trellised passageway beckoning toward an inner courtyard, the mullioned windows in odd little nooks. The entire effect was one of unhurried charm. This was not a house for efficient, no-nonsense living. It was a home where life should be savored and enjoyed one leisurely moment at a time.

They went inside, walking through the empty rooms together, and Danni's plans for the place spilled out: the paneling in the back den that should be replaced with plaster work, the kitchen cabinets that should be stripped and repainted in bright colors, the concrete countertops she had in mind. But then she sensed a restlessness in Bryan, a discontent.

"There's something about this house that bothers you," she said. "Even though you bought it, and it's yours now, you don't seem at home here."

"Yeah, well…it reminds me of all the wrong things." His look was brooding as he gazed out one of the living room windows. "When I was a kid," he said at last, "my mom cleaned houses in her spare time. I didn't know about it at first…didn't know she was hiring herself out as a maid. When I figured it out, I was ticked at my father for leaving us in debt the way he had. And then I was ticked at myself for not being old enough to make everything right." Bryan paused, and then he went on.

"This house is one of the places she worked…the main place, actually. And it's the one that got to me the most. The people who lived here…they treated my mom as if she were somehow less than they were…I saw them…they were condescending and patronizing. And so, when I was thirteen years old, I swore to myself that someday I'd buy this place so my mom could be the lady of the house.''

He shook his head. ''But now it's almost too late. Because she's sick. She's dying.'' Although his voice was perfectly expressionless, Danni heard all the pain behind his words. She went to him.

''Bryan, I'm sorry. Terribly sorry.''

''She's a tough old bird. Not always easy to get along with. But she cleaned this damn house for years. I wanted to surprise her with it, remodel it into something new for her.''

Danni put her arms around him and held him fiercely. ''You'll do it. There still has to be time.''

''I don't know, Danni.''

She went on holding him, everything forgotten now but the need to provide comfort. For the second time, she was the one who initiated a kiss. Tentative at first, exploring… She twined her fingers in his hair, and molded herself closer to him, wanting to obliterate the sadness she sensed in him.

With unthinking provocativeness she arched against him, inciting a response. His tongue probed her mouth, his hands moved along her back as if he needed to feel every part of her. Oh, she needed it too....

Madness. Nothing can truly be this good. It has to stop.

But she couldn't stop. This was what she'd been wanting since the very first time he'd kissed her. Her fingers shook as she tugged his shirt from his jeans, seeking his bare flesh. He groaned, all the encouragement she needed.

"Danni," he murmured, his voice husky. "I told myself that I'd wait. That you weren't ready for this, after all..."

She didn't listen. Boldly, she undid the snap of his jeans, slid the zipper downward...realized just what a response she'd provoked.

"Danni..."

She kicked off her shoes, then pushed her own jeans and brief undergarment down her legs. Only her blouse provided the skimpiest of cover. But soon that too came unbuttoned, opened to reveal her lacy camisole. Bryan cupped her breasts, his fingers caressing her through the soft material until she almost cried out. A moment later he knelt before her and pressed his mouth against her. Now she *did* cry out, astounded at the sudden waves of pleasure pulsing through her. How could it have happened so quickly, so wantonly...

"Let yourself go," he murmured, understanding. Afterward he drew her down beside him to the floor. They pillowed themselves on their discarded clothes. Danni tugged impatiently at his briefs until at last he was fully revealed to her. How she ached to have him deep inside her. And so she showed him what she needed, opening to him, putting her hand on him and guiding him into her.

They gazed at each other as they rocked together, Danni's legs wrapped fiercely around Bryan, her flesh melding with his. And then, all over again, she gasped with the cascades of pleasure, his moans telling her of his own fulfillment.

An endless moment later they lay tangled together, the early evening sunlight warming them through the windows. Danni wondered at her brazenness. She made no move to cover herself, reveling in the way Bryan's gaze traveled over her. Apparently he hadn't yet had enough of her.

"Beautiful," he murmured, leaning over to kiss the hollow of her throat. She was completely, uncomplicatedly happy. All the questions, all the confusion of the past few days seemed to have vanished. What had happened between them was so right…so inevitable. Somehow they would work everything out—she was convinced of it. And, meanwhile, she traced her fingers over the swirl of dark hair on his chest.

"Danni…do you want to get me started again?" His voice was huskier than ever.

"I think it's a distinct possibility." She gazed speculatively at his very masculine body, assessing the signs of a repeat performance. He kissed her, laughing gently.

"Hey, I do have to get my strength back."

"Something tells me it won't be a problem." She needed a lifetime of being with him like this, knowing she would never tire of his touch. Yes, somehow they would work it all out….

"Today was much better, wasn't it?" he murmured.

"Hmm…better than what?" she asked lazily.

"Better than the other night. Maybe now you'll believe me when I tell you how sexy you are."

Danni stilled. An icy coldness seemed to drench her. "The other night," she repeated with a dawning sense of horror.

"Yes," he said in an amused tone. "In my bed."

Damn Kristine. Damn her. Danni's stomach churned. She grabbed her shirt and her pants, struggled into them.

"Danni, what the hell is wrong?"

Now Danni's horror was complete. Kris obviously hadn't talked to Bryan, after all. She hadn't confessed. Instead she'd *slept* with the man.

"Bryan, I think you'd better get dressed." Danni was surprised at the calmness of her voice, the steadiness of her hands as she found her last few items of clothing. Bryan frowned, but he slipped on his jeans.

"Okay, what is this all about?" he demanded.

She took a deep breath, steeling herself. "Bryan, I have a sister."

He shrugged. "Lots of people have sisters."

"A...twin sister."

He studied her, face impassive. That terrible coldness seemed to weigh down on her, but she managed to speak again.

"Bryan, you've...met her."

He was getting the picture now. She could see it in his eyes. But his expression was still unreadable as his gaze raked over her. She would have preferred his anger, his outrage. Anything but that look pinning her as if she were some helpless, pathetic creature.

She didn't know how long they would have remained like this, frozen in a dreadful tableau. But then the front door opened and heels clicked across the oak floor.

"Bryan? Bryan, I hope you're here—" Kristine appeared in the arch to the living room. And then she, too, froze as she glanced from Bryan to Danni and then back again. And Bryan faced both of them.

Identical twin sisters.

CHAPTER SIX

BRYAN FELT as if he'd suddenly walked into a carnival house of mirrors…glass fracturing to produce a multitude of images. Well, two images to be exact. Two Dannis. One of them glared at the other.

"I can't believe it, Kris. I can't believe you'd outright lie to me. You said you'd *told* him. You swore you had—"

The other one looked miserable. "I intended to tell him. I truly did…but then…it felt so good to be wanted…."

"So you pretended to be me again. And you…you went to bed with him…." This Danni's face was ashen.

"I knew it was wrong. Terribly wrong. But I felt so alone—"

"Nothing can excuse what you did, Kris."

Not two Dannis, of course. A Kris and a Danni. That was helpful. The real Danni, it seemed, was the one he'd held in his arms only a few moments ago. But right now the only way he could tell her apart was the clothes she wore—jeans and a shirt that remained only half-buttoned. The other Danni—Kris—looked more sophisticated. A dress, high heels.

He continued to watch as if this were happening to someone else. Because it sure as hell couldn't be happening to *him.* Falling for one beautiful blonde…finding out there were two beautiful blondes. Apparently he'd been… snookered. Confronting that fact, all he felt right now was a strange numbness.

"What the hell kind of game were you playing?" he asked. "The subterfuge, and all."

The sophisticated blonde turned to him earnestly, but didn't seem able to speak.

"Why didn't you tell me?" he addressed his question to the real Danni.

"I should have," she said, her voice expressionless. "Right from the minute I found out. But…I thought she… My mistake."

"Oh, Danni," Kris whispered. "Will you ever forgive me? And will you believe that the reason I came here today…was to finally tell Bryan the truth…"

"It's a little late for that, isn't it?" Danni asked, her voice still completely devoid of emotion. She turned back to Bryan. "I'm sorry," she said with considerable dignity. "I wish you hadn't had to go through any of this. Believe me, I don't have any excuses for my part in it. I'm just...sorry." With that, she grabbed her shoes and strode out the door. Which left him with only one blonde—Kris. She stood there for a moment, the expression on her face revealing some inner struggle.

"Bryan, I wish you could forgive me now—this very instant. That way I wouldn't feel so terrible. But it's too much to ask, isn't it?" She shook her head sorrowfully. "I wouldn't blame you if you hated me. The funny thing is, though...I still don't regret the way I feel about you. I don't regret it one bit." Now she was the one who exited, her heels clicking over the wooden floor.

Which left Bryan with no blonde at all.

BRYAN ORDERED another beer.

"Trying to get drunk?" Robert Serna asked him conversationally.

"That's kind of the idea." So far, it wasn't working.

"Twins, eh?" This from Robert.

"Twins," Bryan repeated. He and Robert sat

in a dark, smoky bar in downtown San Diego. The two of them had known each other for years—seen each other through the ups and downs of their personal and professional careers. It seemed natural for Bryan to confide in his closest friend.

"Well, you know," Robert said. "Some guys have fantasies about twins."

Bryan gave him a sour glance.

"I guess you're pretty ticked," Robert said. "At both of them."

"Both of them—one of them—who the hell knows," Bryan muttered. "I don't even know if I can tell the two of them apart."

"The one I met," Robert said, "seemed nice...very nice!"

Bryan gave him another dour look.

"Just go on being ticked," Robert said. "Can't say I blame you."

Too bad being ticked didn't solve anything. And too bad it didn't stop him thinking about Danni Ferris.

Except that he didn't even know who Danni was.

IT WAS THE BIG DAY, Monday after Thanksgiving, time to pitch the presentation to Hobbyhorse

Toys. But Danni's world had turned to ashes. Did one client more or less matter?

''Danni, didn't you hear me?'' Michelle asked. ''Where are the slides? Mr. Nolan expects us to use Power Point slides. I don't want to disappoint him.''

Larry made a sound that could only be called skeptical. Michelle frowned.

''Mr. Nolan has very high standards. He believes in excellence. I happen to believe in excellence, too.''

Larry made another expressive sound. Michelle squinted at him suspiciously. And Danni turned to stare unseeing out the window of her office.

Someday Larry would realize the silliness of loving Michelle. Someday Michelle would realize the futility of loving Mr. Nolan, senior partner of Nolan, Williams and Beck. And someday, perhaps, Danni would be able to forget the expression on Bryan's face yesterday. No overdrawn emotion, no overplayed reaction when he'd learned the truth...just a hard, grim, unforgiving look.

''Danni,'' Michelle said, sounding panicked.

Danni turned from the window. ''The overheads are in that folder on the cabinet, exactly where they should be. We're on time...let's go.'' She walked down the corridor to the conference room, Michelle on one side, Larry on the other. The two of them put on their business faces—bland, smiling masks. Danni made a supreme effort to do the same.

Fifteen minutes later, she was fully aware that the meeting was not going well. Storyboards, slides, all the right technical equipment—and it still wasn't working. The ideas were all wrong. Uninspired, ordinary. Flat. Suddenly Danni felt impatient with the whole thing. With a clatter, she set down the pointer she'd been using. Michelle and Larry sent her alarmed glances, but she ignored them. She addressed the row of Hobbyhorse executives on the other side of the conference table.

''Look,'' she said. ''You know what's really important in life? Building something...creating something to last. On some level, everyone wants that. So here's what we do. We let your customers build. We let them create.'' A new idea was forming even as she spoke, carrying her along and stirring her at last from her dismal lethargy. She placed her hands on the table, leaning forward just a little. ''We hold a city-wide competition. We have a contest to see who can build the most original and inventive...rocking horse. A fitting symbol for Hobbyhorse Toys. The winner will be announced on Christmas Eve, with all the celebratory fanfare. And we'll encourage any and all rocking horses to be distributed to children's charities around town."

Michelle looked aghast. Larry merely looked worried. But the row of executives had perked up. Danni saw nods, heard interested murmurs.

"She just may have something.... Interesting way to advertise who we are...makes us look good at the same time... A little Christmas spirit never hurt anybody...."

The rest of the meeting passed in a blur. At the end of it, Danni was treated to a series of enthusiastic handshakes. Nolan, Williams and Beck had unanimously won the Hobbyhorse account. The executives filed out, leaving Danni with her team.

"I believe," said Michelle, "that Mr. Nolan is going to be very happy about this."

Larry groaned.

"Stop, both of you," said Danni. "We don't have a minute to lose—we're going to be working on this thing day and night. Larry, get cracking on the draft for the newspaper ads. Michelle, you'll sketch the layout. That's just for starters. Any kind of personal life between now and Christmas—you might as well forget it.'' She felt a welcome surge of energy. Maybe, just maybe, if she worked long enough and hard enough, she would forget that expression on Bryan's face.

Maybe she'd even forget the heartache she felt.

IT WAS LATE that evening when Danni pulled up at Bryan's apartment. She sat in the car for the longest time, clenching the wheel. But this was something that just had to be done—she couldn't delay it any longer. She climbed out of the car and went to Bryan's door.

When he opened it, she finally saw the anger she'd been expecting—and dreading.

''Which one are you?'' he asked. ''Or maybe I'm supposed to guess.''

''It's Danni,'' she said, struggling to speak calmly. ''Listen, Bryan, this won't take long. There are a few things that need saying, and then...I'll be out of here.''

His gaze traveled over her. ''How the hell,'' he said, ''am I supposed to believe you're the real Danni? Maybe this is just another damn setup.''

She shifted her briefcase wearily from one hand to the other. ''It really is me. Bryan...please just let me do what I came here for.''

After a moment he stood aside. ''Be my guest,'' he said.

She stepped into his apartment, barely noticing the surroundings.

''I'm here to offer you a formal apology. And to explain. I think you have a right to know exactly what happened. I'll start at the beginning.''

There was no encouragement from him. He stood there regarding her with that relentless gaze. She swallowed hard and continued.

''Kris ,pretended to be me at that Partner to Partner gala last month. And then apparently she pretended to be me a few more times...with you. When I found out about it, I was furious. I should have told you right off, Bryan, but Kris begged me to let her do it in her own way. And then she swore she *had* told you....'' Danni stopped in frustration. ''This is coming out all wrong,'' she said. ''It sounds as if I'm trying to find excuses, trying to justify myself—''

''Aren't you?'' he asked.

"No...yes. I don't know!" She gripped her briefcase with both hands. "Maybe I shouldn't have trusted my sister to come clean. But, truthfully, I didn't want to be the one to tell you. Because...because I knew how you'd react. How you'd feel. Exactly the way you're feeling now—"

"I don't know what the hell I'm feeling, Danni. So how can you know?"

He wasn't going to make this easy—and who could blame him? She desperately wanted to get it over with, but somehow the right words wouldn't come.

"Maybe I can only imagine what you're thinking," she said. "But part of me wanted Kris to take the blame. The truth is, I'm to blame. Another part hoped that you'd figure it out on your own. That you'd see the differences between us, without any help...maybe that was the real reason I gave Kris those two days. Because I wanted so much for you to see me for who I am—a whole, unique person. Not simply one half of the Ferris twins."

Her confession seemed to have no effect on him; she sensed the hardness still there.

"I'm trying to unravel things," he said at last. "Trying to figure out which one of you I was with...when. Some of the times I know. I tell myself, yeah, that was Danni. Or that was...Kris. But other times—it could have been you. It could have been her. I don't know. And that *does* bug the hell out of me.''

Danni's face burned. ''I know that—''

''I keep asking myself why I couldn't tell the difference. And I keep coming up with no answers,'' Bryan muttered.

Danni gave a bitter smile. ''Maybc there isn't an answer. But you know what's funny? Kris's husband is the only man who's ever really been able to tell us apart. That's one of the reasons I believed Ted was the right one for her. Except that now everything seems to be falling apart in their marriage, and—''

''Lord,'' Bryan said heavily. ''She's married?''

Danni felt a sense of shock. He hadn't known about Ted...of course he hadn't. That was just one more part of Kristine's deception.

''Bryan, I'm sorry—''

''This relationship is getting more crowded all the time. Two sisters. A husband. Why not just invite the entire damn city?''

Everything was just getting worse and worse. ''Bryan, I don't know how many times I can apologize. For me, for Kris. Even though I realize no apology can make it up to you...I'm sorry."

The expression on his face remained unyielding. And, with a despair that settled deep inside her, Danni knew there was nothing more she could say.

ELIZABETH HAD surprised Bryan. After a relapse that had landed her in the hospital, his mother was sitting up, telling the doctors exactly what she thought of them, complaining about the food and demanding to go home. Bryan, despite his better judgment, started to entertain terms like "remission" and "second chances."

The doctors informed him that Elizabeth McKay had merely responded well to adjustments in her pain medications. She could go home only if she had around-the-clock nursing care. Another relapse could occur at any moment, and Bryan shouldn't get his hopes up.

He got his hopes up, anyway. He transported his mother away from the hospital with a maximum of fanfare...knowing that she was secretly pleased with all the fuss.

"Well, at least you don't expect me to move in with you," she grumbled. "I'm spared *that* indignity.'' She spoke regally from the hospital bed Bryan had purchased for her bedroom. Next she made certain that while she'd been gone, he'd cared well for her three cats—Buster, Dots and Oliver. Then she scowled at the male nurse adjusting her IV. When he winked at her, she pretended to be shocked. After he left the room, she shook her head.

''A young man like that should be a doctor, not a nurse, for goodness' sake.''

''Guess everyone's turning the social order upside down,'' Bryan remarked dryly. His mother gave him a sharp look.

''Don't accuse *me* of being old-fashioned, Bryan. I'm perfectly willing to accept novelty—such as that young woman of yours being a carpenter.''

He didn't say anything.

''I'd very much like to meet her,'' his mother continued. ''That is, if she could tolerate all these contraptions around me.''

He didn't say anything for another moment, but then he saw the expression on his mother's face. So hopeful. And she wouldn't give up.

''You said you were serious about her,'' Elizabeth persisted. ''Well, are you?''

So maybe now was the time to tell her. Not

only had he broken up with one beautiful blonde...he'd broken up with two. But the eager expression on his mother's face stopped him.

"I was serious," he said at last.

If she noticed his use of the past tense, she didn't let on. "Something tells me this woman is different, Bryan. Different in a good way from any other woman in your life. It's the tone of your voice when you speak about her...the look in your eyes."

If she only knew, Bryan thought. The situation was certainly different.

"So, if anything is wrong between you and this Danni Ferris, you'd better do something about it," said his mother. "You'd better fix it quick."

"Some things aren't that easy to fix," he said.

She sat up a little straighter against the pillows and stared at him intently. "Don't argue with somebody who doesn't have a whole lot of time left."

"You have time—"

"Cut it out, son," she told him. "You're not convincing me. And you're sure as heck not convincing yourself."

Bryan worked on it the next two days. He looked for signs that his mother was improving.

The fact that she was able to walk into the living room with only a little help, the way she'd eaten a little more than usual at lunch, the phone calls she made to her friends in Saint Louis. He tried to ignore the fact that she paid for every effort. After that foray into the living room, she'd fallen into a long, exhausted sleep. He tried to ignore that she hardly ate anything at all. And he definitely tried to ignore that all her phone calls sounded like farewells.

"Bryan, why haven't you brought her to see me?" his mother asked one night, when he came to her apartment straight from the office.

Danni again. The old gal wasn't going to let up.

"Mom, this isn't exactly the best time—"

"Well, it's the only time I've got," she said irritably, moving her head against the pillows. "Bryan, I want to see at least one thing settled before I go. I want to see *you* settled."

"I'm fine," he said.

She didn't seem to be listening. "Your father...*he* didn't leave anything settled. I swear, sometimes I think I'm still struggling with the fallout. All these years later, and so much is unresolved. If there's anything to that afterlife stuff,'' she continued, her eyelids drifting downward. ''If there's anything to it at all...when I see your father, I'm going to tell him exactly what I think of him. Nothing spared.'' She breathed slowly, evenly, and Bryan was sure she slept. He went to the window, gazing out at the setting sun. Crimson, orange, violet...it was a good show. Too bad it did nothing to solve the emptiness inside him.

''Bryan,'' said his mother from the bed, her voice unexpectedly firm. ''Did you fix it?''

''Fix what?''

''Don't play dumb. Did you fix whatever was wrong with you and your Danni?''

An interesting way to phrase it. He no longer had ''his'' Danni.

''No,'' he said after a minute. ''I didn't fix it.''

''Well, do it. Dying wishes should be taken very seriously. They should be honored.''

He couldn't answer...couldn't speak past the tightness in his throat.

Now Elizabeth did sleep, falling into the exhaustion that overtook her so easily. Bryan watched her for a few more moments, and then he turned back to the sunset. It had deepened, the colors shading toward night. He stood there watching, and thinking. And he knew what he had to do.

CHAPTER SEVEN

"I've left Ted."

Kristine delivered these words quietly and tonelessly as she wheeled her cart down an aisle of the health food emporium in Sugar Beach. Danni wondered if she'd heard right.

"You walked out on him?"

"Don't say it like that! And don't say it so loudly." Kristine grabbed a jar of organic honey, tossed it into her cart and went hurrying along.

"Kris, are you all right?" Always that unwilling concern for her sister. No matter how angry Kristine made her, it always came back to that. Worry...protectiveness.

"Of course I'm all right. This is a step in the right direction, at last." Now a box of organic raisins went flying into the cart. "I finally did something positive, finally realized that my marriage was over—"

"Does Ted know it's over?"

Kristine stopped the cart, gripping the handle with both hands. ''He killed this marriage a long time ago,'' she said. ''I'm not the one who did it.''

''So what did Ted do? Was it another woman? Because I can't think of anything else that would bring you so much hurt—''

''I'm happy, dammit. There's no hurt, not anymore.'' As soon as Kristine said these words, her eyes welled with tears. ''Oh, damn,'' she muttered, pushing the cart along. ''Someone could see me like this. And then they'll all gloat about poor little Kristine, her life in ruins.''

Danni took a bottle of flaxseed oil from the shelf and pretended to read the label. ''Hmm...you don't want anyone to know about your troubles. I guess that's why you're shopping at the neighborhood store where somebody you know is bound to see you.''

''Well, I'm not going to slink.'' Kristine said fiercely. ''I'm sure that's what they all expect.''

Danni sighed. ''If they were really your friends, they'd just want to make you feel better. Of course, you probably haven't given them a chance. You've probably kept them at a distance—just like you've done with me.''

Kristine glanced away. ''Distance...you're

the one who hasn't wanted anything to do with *me.* Today's the first time you've even agreed to see me, or talk to me. I know you despise me, of course, and I can't blame you...."

"Kris, it's no good wallowing. That's just one more way of avoiding responsibility for what you did. All the lies—"

"I'm sorry!" Kristine's voice wavered. "What more can I say? I'm just so terribly sorry."

Those were almost exactly the same words that Danni herself had used with Bryan.

"I'm still trying to understand why you did it," Danni said. "Maybe Ted hurt you so much you were just trying to get back at him—"

"How can you say that?" Kristine demanded. "You think I'd use you—use Bryan—to get revenge on *Ted?*"

"Yeah," Danni said. "That's exactly what I think. Let's just assume Ted had an affair...and you decided you'd have one of your own."

"You make it sound so calculated," Kristine said desolately. "But it wasn't like that. I kept wanting to do the right thing...I kept wanting to tell Bryan the truth...but he had this way of looking at me. As if he could make all the unhappiness and the hurt go away...."

Danni knew that look all too well. She'd gazed into Bryan's eyes and seen it, too. So many emotions threatened to overwhelm her. Anger. Despair. Longing...

"Well, it's over," she said flatly. "Neither one of us has any right to anything Bryan can offer."

For once, Kristine seemed to stir from her self-absorbed misery. She gazed intently at Danni, truly seeming to see her at last. "Oh, Danni. You have it bad," she said in dismay. "You really care about him, don't you? Maybe as much as I do."

If her sister actually started getting sympathetic, Danni knew she'd be undone. She grabbed a bag of chocolate-covered pretzels and lobbed them into the cart.

"This isn't a contest between us! It's not like the time we tried out for that stupid cheerleading squad—"

"And neither one of us made it," Kristine finished.

"Or the time," Danni, said, "we both wanted that one-of-a-kind dress for the senior prom—"

"And we argued about it so long that Lisa Miller bought it right out from under our noses. I get the message," Kristine said wryly. "When you and I compete, Danni, we both end up losing. But this time...this time there's a whole lot more at stake, isn't there? The most wonderful man any woman could hope to know.''

''Stop, Kris! You make it sound as if one of us still had a chance with Bryan! It's over, do you understand? No more tricks. No more lies.''

Kristine stood with her head bowed, her hands clenched on the handle of the cart. ''I can't help wishing for the impossible,'' she said in a low voice. ''With Bryan I could have a new chance. A new life. I could put everything else behind me.''

Danni's impatience flared. But as always, she felt that other emotion too...the love for her sister.

''Kris,'' she said, ''you may not believe it, but I do want you to be happy. I just don't see how you *can* be, if you can even imagine using Bryan to run away from your problems.''

''I know,'' Kristine whispered. ''But still...I can't help dreaming....''

''Well, you have to stop. That's all there is to it.'' With those words, the emptiness inside Danni only deepened. Because she had to stop dreaming, too.

MICHELLE POKED her head inside Danni's office. "That stunning man is out in the lobby," she announced with an air of importance. "You know, the one who was here before."

"Really," Danni mumbled distractedly, sifting through the pile of papers on her desk.

"He's asking for you."

Danni groaned. "Not another one of the suits from Hobbyhorse Toys. Haven't we convinced them by now that we're doing our job?"

"Look, it doesn't matter *where* he's from," Michelle said. "He's almost more handsome than Mr. Nolan."

High praise, indeed. "Well, thanks for sharing," Danni said. "I seem to recall you do have work."

Michelle ignored this broad hint. Instead she glanced down the hall. "Oh, my gosh, here he comes. He looks better the closer he gets."

Danni stifled another groan. She wasn't in the mood for any of this. But then Michelle scuttled aside, and the so-called stunning man appeared in the doorway. Bryan McKay.

Danni's heart gave a jolt, and refused to settle back into its normal rhythm. She pressed a hand to her throat, but that did nothing to soothe her. Bryan gave no greeting, simply gazed at her impassively. He *was* wearing a suit, but—like the man himself—it was not common or ordinary in any way. The right cut, the right fit, the right shade of cinder gray. Understated perfection, as always. Truly nothing but the best for Bryan McKay.

Gradually she became aware of the tense silence, and of the way Michelle was peering with great interest around Bryan. At last Danni found her voice.

''Thanks, Michelle,'' she said pointedly, surprised at how calm she sounded. ''See you later.''

Michelle hovered for another few seconds, then wandered disappointedly away.

''Have a seat, Bryan,'' Danni said, still amazed at her own steadiness. She searched his face. If she expected to find any relenting there...she was disappointed. He was still angry, all right. She could see it in his eyes...a coldness that would probably never thaw.

He sat down across from her desk. She reshuffled some papers. ''Look, Bryan, why are you here? I thought we'd already said everything.''

''Maybe we have a few more things to kick

around,'' he said brusquely. ''But this isn't the place to do it. We need a little privacy.''

''I can't imagine what for—''

''Humor me, Danni.''

''If you're trying to say I owe you something, Bryan—you're right. I owe you an apology. I can't tell you that enough. But—''

''Happens to be a nice day outside. We can go for a walk.''

She rubbed her temples, staring at all the files and papers on her desk. Suddenly she felt stifled in here, and she very much wanted to get out.

She stood and grabbed her purse. ''I can take half an hour.''

''Fine,'' he said cryptically. Together they went down the hall. Michelle craned her neck from her cubicle to watch the two of them go by. Danni frowned at her, but knew there would be no end of speculation about Bryan.

It *was* a nice day outside, one of those lovely San Diego afternoons that could only be described as balmy. The ocean air permeated this downtown district, and the sky was a clear, pastel blue. What a wonderful setting it would be for someone who felt lighthearted...worry-free. Danni wondered if she would ever feel that way again.

"I gather you have something to say to me, Bryan. I'm listening."

"I need you to do a favor for me," he said, his voice expressionless. "A big one. I spoke to my mother about you, back when...back when I thought there was only one of you."

"There *is* only one of me, dammit. I'm not my sister—"

"Just let me get on with it," Bryan said, his voice hard now. "I talked about you, and now my mother's latched on to the idea that we're meant for each other. It seems to be the only thing giving her any hope...any peace. The notion that I'll be settled down soon. So—if that's what she needs, that's what she'll get. I want you to meet her."

Danni kept walking automatically. "I see. Another pretense."

"It won't be for very long."

She knew what his words implied. His mother wouldn't be around much longer. Now she stopped in the middle of the sidewalk and gazed at him intently. "Bryan, I'm sorry about your mom. Terribly sorry. But it would be wrong to deceive her! Hasn't there been enough of that already?"

"She won't know the truth."

"Right," Danni said grimly. "What you don't know can't hurt you...is that the idea?"

"Whatever time she has left, I want her to be happy. And like we said, Danni...you owe me." His face was implacable.

Danni folded her arms against her body. The ache inside her was becoming more and more a physical thing. "Why aren't you asking Kristine to do this for you?"

"She's the one with the husband."

"Only a technicality at this point," Danni told him. "She's separated—"

"I'm not into technicalities." Still that hardness in his voice. "Besides, you're the real Danni Ferris. Let's keep this as uncomplicated as we can."

She gave a hollow laugh. "A little late for that, isn't it? But the answer is no, Bryan. I can't do it. No matter what, it wouldn't be right. Pretending never is."

"Too bad you and your sister didn't think of that earlier."

She took a deep breath. It wouldn't do any good to remind him that Kristine had been the one pretending—not her. Clearly he blamed both of them.

"No more deception," she said. "Your mother deserves better."

"She deserves a little peace."

Danni shook her head. "No, Bryan. I just can't. Deception—for any reason—is wrong. And it always comes back to haunt the deceiver. I'm going back now. And please...don't try to come with me. Don't try to convince me." She turned and walked away. Part of her longed for him to follow. But he didn't. He stayed where he was, and she went all the way back to her office alone.

THAT EVENING the phone was ringing as Danni let herself into her apartment. Could it be Bryan, calling to argue with her? Just to hear the sound of his voice again...

"Hello," she said crisply.

"Is this Danni?" The voice was a female one, a bit impatient.

"Yes, it's Danni."

"This is Elizabeth McKay."

"Who..."

"Elizabeth McKay. Bryan's mother, of course. What's going on between you and my son?"

Danni couldn't think of a word to say. She

felt just the way she had when she was nine years old, and her fourth-grade teacher had caught her out at some mischief. Odd how merely a voice over the telephone wire could do that to her.

"Mrs. McKay," she managed to say at last, "I wish I could tell you—"

"I'm inviting you to dinner at my apartment tomorrow night. Seven-thirty. We'll sort it out then. Please come. I don't have a lot of time to waste, Danni." With that, Elizabeth McKay hung up the phone.

Danni stared at the receiver in perplexity. The woman hadn't sounded like someone dying. Instead she'd sounded like someone very much in control of the situation.

BRYAN'S MOTHER was a fighter. Danni could tell that much right off. Elizabeth McKay came to greet her at the door of her apartment, even though obviously it took great effort. Her face was drawn, her eyes shadowed by illness. And yet she gave Danni a thorough, disconcerting appraisal. Then, after a moment, she gave Danni's hand a squeeze, her grip surprisingly strong.

"It's very good to meet you, dear," she began, then paused. Swaying a bit, she reached out to steady herself against the wall. Danni studied her with concern.

"I don't think you should be up, Mrs. McKay," she said.

"Oh—and what *should* I be doing? Composing my obituary?" Elizabeth started making her way slowly down the hall. "I'm still alive and kicking, you know. I'm not quite as spry as I used to be, perhaps. But I'm alive and kicking."

There was something of a bustle after that, getting Elizabeth settled over her protests. A nurse appeared and somehow convinced her to lie back on the sofa. Elizabeth orchestrated everything from this vantage point, first introducing Danni to her three cats.

"Buster is the orange-and-white one. He likes affection, but only if you pretend not to notice. Dots is short for Dorothy. She may look sweet, but she's perfectly capable of taking Oliver in two out of three...and yes, that's Oliver over there, actually asleep in his basket for once."

Danni was suitably attentive, while all three cats ignored her haughtily. Now Elizabeth waved toward dinner, waiting buffet-style on the table. Danni and the nurse helped themselves, and then clustered around the sofa. Danni liked the fact that Elizabeth insisted on the nurse eating with them.

"*I* should have been the one to cook," Elizabeth grumbled.

"Then you wouldn't have any of my glorious tofu pot pie," said the nurse cheerfully. Her name was Geneva.

"Tofu..." muttered Elizabeth. "I hope you disguised it. Why is everyone suddenly enamored with tofu?"

"It's delicious," Danni told Geneva. It really was good food; too bad Danni's appetite seemed to evade her.

"Ha," said Elizabeth. "You should be here when Matthew does dinner. He brings me hamburgers and French fries."

"Matthew's the other nurse," confided Geneva, "and I'm sorry, but he has *atrocious* taste in food."

Elizabeth objected, and Geneva argued—just as Elizabeth clearly wanted her to. Danni noticed that Elizabeth hardly touched anything on her plate; every effort she made at normalcy was a valiant one. Finally Danni helped to clear the plates.

"Go find something to do," Elizabeth said to Geneva. "I want to talk to Danni."

Obligingly the nurse disappeared.

"Forget she's here," said Elizabeth. "You and I will just have a chat."

Danni's gaze kept straying toward the paintings on the wall—generic landscape prints, the kind that come with a furnished rental, no matter how elegant the rental might be.

"Now, tell me all about it," Elizabeth said, leaning her head back against the pillows. "Why do you and my son seem to be having trouble?"

Danni felt as if she'd stumbled onto a theater stage. It was time to say her lines and she was panicking. She tried to focus her attention on those generic prints, but Bryan's mother was waiting.

Danni turned back to Elizabeth, clearing her throat. "Well, you see...it's rather an awkward situation. The fact of the matter is, Mrs. McKay..." Despite what Bryan would no doubt have to say, Danni had come here tonight to clear the air—end this unfortunate charade once and for all with the truth. She'd made up her mind to make a clean breast of the situation with Elizabeth.

"You love him, don't you, dear," Elizabeth said with a faint sparkle in her eyes.

Danni could only stare at her. "Love...I hardly think..."

"No use denying it. Of course my Bryan is such an easy man to love. Did you know that he was all A's in high school? And I don't even know how he found time to study, what with football practice and basketball practice. Both his teams took state his senior year."

"A regular paragon," Danni murmured.

Elizabeth's eyes sparkled all the more. "You don't fool me, dear. You can't wait to hear more stories about him."

The woman was exasperating—and very perceptive.

"He won a full scholarship to college," Elizabeth continued. "Not just for sports, but based on his academic achievement. He'd scarcely graduated from college when he got an offer from a prestigious firm in New York. Financial services, management consulting, you know the type of thing. Except that Bryan couldn't be satisfied working for someone *else* very long. He came back to San Diego and went into business for himself after only a few years, and he's been very successful ever since. And how could he not be? He has a very dynamic, charismatic personality."

Elizabeth grew more subdued. "Of course, there is something driving Bryan's success. He's been trying very hard to prove that he's not like his father. Bryan hated all the debt, all the money worries Randall left us with. He decided he would make up for all of it. And he has...a hundredfold. Only he doesn't seem to realize it yet. He seems to think there is always something more he should be doing. Plus, he keeps things bottled up inside way too much. And he always wants to be in control of everything."

Danni listened in reluctant fascination. She could very well have gone on listening—but just then the topic of conversation himself entered the apartment. Bryan.

Danni felt oddly breathless all of a sudden. She was glad that one of the cats had finally decided to grace her with his presence. Buster, the orange-and-white one, stood in front of her and allowed her to tickle one ear. When she finally ventured a glance at Bryan, she gathered that he was not pleased to see her here on her own. But, it was just as his mother said—he kept himself under control.

"Hello, Danni," he said, pulling up a chair.

"Hello, Bryan." Now she held out her hand for inspection as Dots came strolling over to her.

''Look at that, son,'' Elizabeth said. ''The cats approve of her. They don't pay that much attention to *you.*''

Bryan got a sour look. ''I'm sure Danni's flattered.'' The sarcasm was obvious.

''Actually, I am.''

They gazed at each other, the unspoken tension pulsing between them. His eyes were so very dark, and so very unyielding at the same time....

With an effort, Danni glanced away. Now, at last, she had another chance to come clean. She had to gather her courage, and not waste the opportunity.

''Bryan, in case you're wondering...I came here tonight because your mother asked me. And I think she wants to learn the truth from me—''

''Right. The truth.'' Bryan took over easily. ''You're going to tell her all about our problems. And Mom, no doubt, will tell you that we're both just nervous about...getting serious. She'll say we have cold feet, and we should get over it.'' As Bryan's gaze held Danni's once again, the message was clear: *Don't you dare tell my mother the real story. Let her keep her illusions. She's too fragile for anything else.*

Against her will, Danni nodded almost imperceptibly. She turned back to Elizabeth. "I suppose that *is* what you'd tell us," she said gently. "That we're both just nervous."

"People with any sense always *are* terrified when they fall in love," Elizabeth said. She seemed to be struggling against sleep, and losing. "I do wish we could talk about it some more...." Her eyes closed.

The nurse came out and spoke in a whisper. "She's had enough for the evening. Don't worry, Mr. McKay, I'll make sure she's as comfortable as possible."

Bryan nodded curtly and ushered Danni from the apartment. Once they were outside in the foyer, the door closed, he frowned at her.

"This isn't exactly what I had in mind," he said.

"No doubt you wanted something carefully scripted," she retorted. "But your mother called me up and asked me here. I couldn't very well say no."

"You could have told me about it," he pointed out.

"Where you're concerned, I always do the wrong thing," she said impatiently. "But I wanted to tell her the truth—and I knew you'd try to stop me. You *did* stop me, unfortunately."

"You've met her now," he said in the brusque tone that was becoming all too familiar. "Do you think she could have handled the truth?"

"I think she might just surprise you. Too bad you didn't give her the chance...too bad I gave in." Danni pushed open the double glass doors leading outside. "Goodbye, Bryan." She hoped those words had the finality they deserved. But it seemed he wasn't done with her just yet.

"You still owe me, Danni. I want you to go somewhere with me."

"Do you think that's such a good idea?" she asked, battling a potent combination of reluctance and longing.

"Humor me," he said.

CHAPTER EIGHT

THE WALLS of the old mission basilica rose a glimmering white in the darkness, a simple cross crowning the tower of five bells. Over two centuries ago the Spanish friars had come to San Diego, traveling the long hard road from Baja California. The fervor of their beliefs had survived fire, earthquake and the ravages of time, and seemed to echo still in this hushed place. Danni wandered with Bryan on the outskirts of the gardens.

"I'm glad you brought me here," she said. "It's a perfect place to put things into perspective."

"Sometimes," he muttered. Danni sensed the restlessness coiled deep inside him.

"Maybe," she said, "you're wondering what your mom and I talked about. Mainly, she wanted to tell me what a stellar person you are."

"Don't trust anything she says," Bryan replied. "Her goal in life has been to keep me from getting what she calls a swelled head."

"Because your father had a swelled head?"

No answer to that.

"That was something else she talked about," Danni continued after a moment. "She says you've spent your whole life trying as hard as you can not to be like your father, and that's why you're so successful. Except that you don't know when to quit."

Bryan said something under his breath that Danni couldn't quite catch, but his impatience was clear.

"I guess that's why you weren't pleased to find me alone with her," she said. "You must have known we'd end up talking about you. And maybe you were afraid I'd find out too much about you."

They kept walking. Bryan guarded his silence, and Danni guarded her own thoughts. She wondered how many passions and sorrows and perplexities this old mission had endured. Her own aching restlessness threatened to engulf her. She wondered if she would ever forget Elizabeth McKay's words. *You love him, don't you, dear...*

Bryan's silence was becoming forbidding. Danni felt compelled to speak.

"The anger's eating you up, isn't it?" she said. "I guess you think my sister and I made a fool of you. Maybe that's the part you can't forgive, most of all. But I just keep wishing you'd see that I tried to handle things the best way I could. Futile, of course—"

He didn't answer. Instead, he turned and took Danni in his arms. They embraced for a long moment, the ancient mission serving as silent witness. Danni was the one who broke away at last, breathing unsteadily.

"Why?" Bryan asked.

She trembled with her need for him, but she kept her distance. "I can feel the anger underneath," she whispered. "Even when you kiss me...I feel it."

He made another sound of frustration under his breath. "Okay, you want me to say I'm angry? Sure, I'm angry that your sister pulled her lousy stunt on me. And I'm angry at you for being so damn loyal to her. That's what kept you from telling me the truth right from the beginning."

She stared at him through the darkness. "That was good, Bryan. You almost let go there for a minute."

"Letting go doesn't do any good," he said tersely. "It doesn't solve any problems."

"Maybe I'm not a problem to be solved," she told him. "Maybe I'm just somebody you need to...leave behind." She took a deep breath. "Maybe I'm mad at you too, Bryan. Maybe I'm mad that you never really saw *me.* And maybe you never really saw Kris, either. Maybe you couldn't tell us apart because you were just creating some image in your mind of a woman you wanted. And maybe neither one of us could ever possibly live up to that ideal. Neither one of us was *real* to you, Bryan. And I think...I think that's what hurts the most." She was angry, all right. Angry at herself and at him, and at everything that had happened. But he was right about one thing—letting go didn't do any good at all. She'd finally said everything, but she still felt a terrible hollowness inside.

Bryan had no answer for her. This time his silence told her the truth: he couldn't argue with anything she'd said.

"I'll take you home," he said at last, his voice carefully expressionless once more. But even this was a problem.

"I left my car at your mother's place—remember?"

"Right, right," he muttered. So he drove her back to Elizabeth McKay's apartment building, and Danni felt a new wave of guilt as she glanced up at Elizabeth's window, darkened now. Bryan's mother thought the two of them were romantically involved. It felt wrong to deceive her. But that was what Bryan had wanted—deception in a good cause.

Danni was relieved to unlock the door of her hatchback. Before she could slip into the driver's seat, however, Bryan came to her. And he kissed her yet again, leaning her against the car. She responded with all the desire and yearning inside her. She was like someone whose thirst could never be quenched. But this moment, too, had to end…and she was the one who ended it.

"No," she said in a shaky voice. "It's no use, Bryan. I think I know why you wanted to be with me tonight. You're trying to figure out the differences between me and Kris. You think that if you kiss me, or touch me, it'll all become clear. But you're still too angry. And it's just…too late."

Once again he had no answer for her. Using the very last remnants of her willpower, Danni climbed into her car and drove away. Glancing in her rearview mirror, she saw him standing there...watching her go. And the emptiness inside her only grew.

"WOMAN PROBLEMS?" asked C. J. Whitfield sympathetically.

"Something like that," Bryan said.

The two of them were sitting in one of San Diego's morc prestigious nightclubs. C.J. had called him, requesting a meeting, and here he was. She seemed to have more than business on her mind. Right now it didn't really matter to him one way or the other.

She angled her stool so that when she crossed her legs, the toe of her high-heeled shoe grazed his leg. Why the hell did women wear spindly shoes like that, anyway? Danni never did, and admittedly he liked that. You wanted to be with a woman who could get a good stride going. Danni's sister, on the other hand, was definitely the high-heel type.

He kept comparing the two of them, looking for differences, cataloguing them...trying to figure out why the differences hadn't clued him in from the beginning. Maybe Danni was right about what she'd said last week. Maybe he'd just invented an ideal woman, something that had never been real, and then expected Danni to live up to it. Danni…or her sister.

"She must be something," C.J. said, "for you to be thinking about her all the time."

They were both something, all right. Bryan drank his beer.

"Perhaps I *will* invest in that project of yours," C.J. said. "How else can I get your attention?"

He made an effort to look at her—really look at her. Maybe his problem was that he just didn't pay enough attention to the little details about a woman. No time like the present to start. C.J. was, undeniably, very attractive. Brunette, hazel eyes, nice figure.

"Let's dance," she murmured.

He supposed he didn't mind the idea. Music, a dance floor, a beautiful woman. The combination seemed right.

She moved into his arms, rested her head against his shoulder. He told himself that it felt nice to be like this with a woman…a woman who hopefully didn't have a twin sister hiding somewhere.

They danced for a little while, and then C.J. made her next move.

"Bryan, do you want to go to my place?"

He supposed he didn't mind that idea, either. They left in separate cars, but Bryan followed C.J. to her house. It turned out to be a long, low, rambling place on the bay, a beach bungalow that seemed to have gotten a little out of control. Bryan didn't like it, right off. It was too stylized, too self-consciously rustic. When C.J. let the two of them inside, he saw pieces of furniture in weathered wood, a quilt thrown artfully over a sofa, a display of seashells. He doubted that C.J. had gathered the shells herself, or that she had made the quilt. It all seemed done for careless effect, but the careless part wasn't working.

She turned the stereo on. ''We could keep dancing,'' she said. ''I'd like that.''

He wasn't exactly in the mood to waltz C. J. Whitfield around her living room. ''I'll pass,'' he said.

She turned the stereo down. ''Just tell me what you want, Bryan. We can do anything...anything at all.''

She made it sound as if they had all the choices in the world. Lately, though, his options hadn't thrilled him. He paced the room.

''Bryan...I could take your mind off her, if only you'd give me a chance.'' She went to a doorway, paused and glanced at him. "I don't believe in being coy. The bed's in here."

At this moment, no one could accuse C. J. Whitfield of being mysterious.

"It can't hurt, Bryan. And maybe it'll even help."

He wasn't convinced—he didn't know if anything would help. But, what the hell.

Bryan started to follow C.J. through the bedroom door, but changed his mind in mid-stride. What the hell was he thinking?

He left her apartment with Danni on his mind.

DANNI LOWERED her head wearily onto her desk. "Less than two weeks till Christmas," she mumbled. "I honestly don't know if we'll make it—this ad campaign might just be the end of us."

"Hey," Larry said, "you sure you're okay, Danni? You seem kind of sick."

That was how she felt, all right…kind of sick. Nothing really serious, just a dragged-down feeling that she couldn't seem to shake. She was always tired lately, overwhelmed by a desire simply to sleep and escape the tumult of her emotions.

"I'm fine," she said unenthusiastically.

"You don't look fine."

"Thank you, Larry," she muttered. "Just what a woman wants to hear."

Michelle came quietly into the office and slid onto a seat. She huddled there as if trying to disappear. This wasn't like her at all—usually she marched into Danni's office as if planning a corporate takeover.

"What's eating you?" asked Larry.

Michelle scrunched down even further in her chair. "It's too horrible," she said in a small voice. "I—I finally got up the courage to tell Mr. Nolan how I felt about him...and he *smiled* at me and said I was just...just a silly kid. Those were his exact words. 'Silly kid.' I am so...humiliated!"

"Well, what did you expect?" Larry asked reasonably. Michelle ducked her head. Danni had never seen her this subdued before. It was disconcerting, to say the least.

"Michelle," Danni said as gently as possible. "If you'd like, you can go home early. It might be good to get away from..."

"The scene of the crime," Larry finished for her.

Michelle finally showed some life. She jerked her head up and glared at him. "Oh, I'm sure it's all very *funny* to you. *You* didn't just make a complete idiot of yourself. Go ahead, say it. 'I told you so.'''

''Hey,'' Larry said, sounding gruff. ''Everybody makes an idiot of themselves now and then.''

''Not *me,*'' Michelle declared. ''At least, not until *now.* Oh, Danni...what am I going to do?''

Danni was the last person in the world to offer advice on matters of the heart. She didn't have any solutions for Michelle—but it seemed she had to try.

''As far as Mr. Nolan,'' she said, ''you'll just have to act like it never happened. You'll be tempted to offer apologies, explanations...but just *don't.* He wants to forget about it. You have to do the same.''

''But I can't forget,'' Michelle said. ''I—I *love* him! And I can't help it if I love him!''

''Get real,'' Larry muttered, looking pained. Danni sighed. Michelle *was* making a fool of herself. Just as Danni had done with Bryan?

''Larry,'' Danni said, ''take Michelle down to the lunch room and get her some coffee. And I saw a couple of Danish in there, too. That ought to do some good.''

"I can't eat...not possibly...and I don't need a *nurse*maid...."

Danni heard Michelle protesting all the way down the hall. At this rate, everyone in the building would soon know about the unfortunate encounter with Mr. Nolan. Michelle was only digging herself in deeper. But, again, Danni could sympathize.

She hadn't seen Bryan for several days now—not since the night at his mother's. He hadn't called, hadn't tried to contact her in any way. And why on earth should he? Perhaps it was really over.

Except for one very important detail Danni had been trying to ignore. She'd been trying to push it out of her mind. But there was still something she had to do, before she said goodbye to Bryan once and for all.

She could no longer delay. Even now, as she sat here, time was running out.

BRYAN WANDERED through the house he'd bought...still wondering why he'd bought it. The idea now seemed pointless. He'd thought that somehow, if he restored this place and surprised his mother with it, he'd make up for all those years she'd struggled. But now he realized he couldn't possibly make up for the past.

He heard a sound and turned. Danni stepped across the threshold of the house, pausing when she saw him.

"You really shouldn't leave the door open," she said briskly. "You never know who's going to walk in."

"Hello, Danni," he said. As usual, there'd been that first moment when he'd had to stop and make sure which Ferris twin it really was. Danni...he knew it from the way she moved, the easy, graceful way she held herself. She looked good...more than good. She wore shorts, a sleeveless shirt, work boots and her tool belt. She looked strong and self-sufficient and sexy.

He kept wanting to be angry at Danni...kept wanting to blame both her and her sister. That way he could be done with both of them. But an inconvenient sense of fairness kept intruding. He had to admit that Danni wasn't the one who'd pulled the stunt. She'd been deceived, too. Only...where did that leave him? Still wondering what the hell he felt about her...

"How are you?" he asked now.

"Bryan, you don't have to make small talk. I'm here on...business."

"Business," he repeated.

"Yes. Business." She seemed determined to rush on. "The original idea was for me to remodel this house. I'd still like the job."

He rubbed his neck. "Doesn't seem like there's much point to it anymore."

"For your mom's sake," Danni said, "it should be done. I've given it a lot of thought, Bryan." Her expression was determined. "After meeting your mother, it just became very clear to me that you need to go through with your plan. You need to give this house to her. And I...well, maybe I need to do something to make up for everything that's happened. Maybe that's the only way *I* can put this whole thing behind me, and move on."

"So you want to pay for your and your sister's sins," Bryan remarked.

"You make Kris and me sound like...like bad people. But we're not. Just confused and upset, and... Anyway, I have it all figured out. I can remodel this place...but you don't have to have much contact with me. We can communicate by fax or e-mail when necessary."

"The miracle of modern technology," Bryan said. "Do you really think I don't want to see you, Danni?"

She gazed at him defensively. "That's the general impression I've been getting."

He'd been hard on her, he knew that. But right now his life felt like a puzzle where the pieces didn't match. He kept moving them around, kept trying to find the right combination. And still nothing fit.

"I don't think this house is important anymore," he said. "Not to my mother."

"That's where you're wrong. She needs to know what you planned for her. You're so important to her, Bryan...she just needs to know."

He didn't agree—but he didn't argue, either. Maybe he wanted an excuse for Danni to hang around. It surprised him how much he wanted her to stay. So he let her bring in a roll of blueprints from her car, and he let her tell him all about her plans for the house. He watched her take measurements...watched her face light up as she talked about beveled corners and biscuit joints, fanlights and friezes. But, most of all, he thought about kissing her.

"Bryan," she said at last, glancing at him in exasperation. "I don't think you've been listening to a single word. I just told you I wanted to knock down that wall, and you hardly blinked."

"Thought you wanted to tear through the place on your own."

She looked around reflectively. "What you need is...well, a vision for the house. And then I'd fulfill the vision for you."

Her choice of words struck him. A vision...that's what he liked about the San Diego-Tijuana project he was working on. Robert and the other architects had a vision. Too bad he didn't have one for his personal life.

"You've got enough ideas for both of us," he told Danni. "I'll just let you do whatever the hell you want with the place. I don't much care what you decide."

She frowned. "You keep acting like you despise this house."

She was right. He couldn't seem to get rid of the memories here. "I remember one time when I was a kid," he said slowly. "I guess I was thirteen or fourteen, and my mother was still cleaning this place every week. She had to come help out during a big party, and I came with her. We stacked drinks on trays, picked up empty glasses, that sort of thing. And the whole time the guests—even the owner of the house—acted as if we were invisible. Less than invisible, really."

"Well," said Danni, "you're certainly not invisible *now.*"

They gazed at each other for a long moment. At last Bryan stepped toward her. He saw a flush rise in her cheeks. She folded her arms and took a step back from him.

"Dammit, Bryan," she said. "Do you think sex is the solution for everything?"

"Depends on who it's with," he said.

"I'm serious."

"So am I," he said.

She shook her head with an odd weariness. "It wouldn't be enough. Especially after everything...everything that's happened. All I want to do is remodel this house for you and your mother, and then—somehow move on."

"Right. I almost forgot. The idea is to pay for your sins...and then start fresh."

She looked displeased, as if she didn't like his choice of words. "Bryan, can't we just get going?"

"You want to start knocking down walls right now?" he asked.

She sighed. "No, of course not. I just...I just want to *resolve* everything." She looked unhappy. It was that overcast look she'd had the first time he'd met her. Correction—the first time he'd met her sister. This was the kind of stuff that really messed with his mind. Recalling something about Danni, and then realizing he'd actually been remembering Kristine. It was like walking on quicksand, never trusting your next move.

Danni was taking out her tape measure again.

"Relax," Bryan said. "You've done enough work for one day. I might have something in the kitchen to eat."

"No," she said decisively. "I'm not hungry."

"Something to drink?"

She hesitated, then gave a reluctant nod. "Thanks. That sounds all right."

He led the way to the kitchen. Here was one of the few substantial pieces of furniture in the house—an old pine table. It had been left behind by the last occupant of the house. Bryan planned to get rid of it.

He opened the fridge, another relic left behind. "Ice water," he said. "A couple of sodas. Beer—"

"Don't even mention beer," she said, pressing a hand to her stomach. "A soda, I guess."

He took out a can, popped the lid and handed

it to her. She sat down on a fold-out metal chair and sipped cautiously.

"Aren't you feeling well?" he inquired.

"It's nothing," she answered, dismissive again.

He sat down in another chair, studying her.

"Bryan, do you have to watch me?" she asked irritably.

"I was just wondering," he said, "what it's like to have a twin."

She set down her soda, and the unhappy look came back. "I should have known," she muttered. "You're thinking about *her.*"

"Guess you answered my question."

Another flush. "Okay, I know how that sounded. Like I'm…jealous of Kris. And in some ways maybe I am. She's always seemed to be the things I'm *not.* A risk taker…embracing life." Danni shrugged. "But we're much the same, too. We're so close, we often make the same choices without even realizing we're doing it." Now she gave him a defiant glance. "We both chose *you,* didn't we? In a manner of speaking."

He rubbed his neck again. "Lord…twins," he muttered.

"Believe me, this whole situation is not something I'd wish on anybody,'' Danni burst out. ''If only we could all just forget about it!'' She stood up quickly, as if to leave. But then, her face white, she swayed and grabbed the edge of the table. Bryan was next to her in a second, easing her back down into the chair.

''Hey,'' he said, ''something really is the matter.''

''Just a little faintness,'' she mumbled. ''Got up too quickly...''

''Danni, you should see a doctor.''

She tried to wave him away. ''I'm fine. Just fine.''

''You're sure as hell not fine.''

She sat there, a strange look passing over her face. ''Oh, no,'' she whispered. She turned from him, propping her face in her hands. ''Just let me sit for a minute,'' she said, her voice suddenly expressionless. Then, after only a few seconds, she stood up again. This time she moved slowly and carefully.

''There—see? I really am fine. And I do have to go now, Bryan. There's something that I have to do right away.''

''I'll go with you,'' he said.

''No. All I need right now is a little time

alone." There was something in her voice that prevented further argument.

And so, against his better judgment, he let her go.

CHAPTER NINE

DANNI WALKED through the aisles of the drugstore, telling herself that this would all turn out to be a huge mistake. The conclusion she had reached while sitting at Bryan's kitchen table some twenty minutes ago could not possibly be an accurate one. She was only a little late...her nausea could be blamed on stress...everybody got dizzy now and then...

Especially if they were pregnant.

No, she told herself firmly. It simply wasn't possible. Very well, she'd been careless that day with Bryan. Extremely careless, if she was going to be honest about it. She hadn't given birth control a thought. She'd simply allowed herself to be swept away by passion and desire and longing....

That was how people got pregnant.

It had only been a few weeks ago, she reasoned with herself. Far too soon to be having symptoms, even if…no ifs, she told herself. Don't even think it.

She had reached the shelf of home pregnancy kits. There were several to choose from. Apparently a booming business, the home pregnancy test. Apparently there were women all over the country just as anxious as she was to know the truth. Of course, many would be hoping for a positive result, but there'd be others like her—women trying to convince themselves that one little lapse could not possibly result in a major life upheaval.

One major lapse.

She grabbed several kits and headed to the front of the store. Did she imagine it, or did the woman at the cash register give her a sympathetic glance? She paid for her purchases and hurried out to her car. If she could just get to her apartment, and find out that she was only imagining her symptoms. Perhaps a touch of flu…

Danni got to her apartment, locked herself safely inside. She felt foolish. She was behaving as if she were a criminal. Next thing she knew, she'd be pulling down the blinds and refusing to answer the telephone if it rang.

The telephone didn't ring. There was nothing

to distract Danni as she opened the paper bag from the drugstore. Fingers trembling, she picked up one of the boxes and read the directions. So simple. So easy. Too easy, perhaps. Finding out whether or not your entire life was about to explode should require more effort.

She stood there for a long moment, feeling as if she balanced on the dividing line between "before" and "after." Oh, how she wanted to stay with "before." But, at last, she ripped the box open. And she followed the directions.

The result was positive. She tried another one of the kits. Positive again.

First came the joy—unreasoning, unexpected.

And then the terror.

"TED IS BEING more than generous," Kristine said in a denigrating tone. "He thinks if he throws money at me, he can make up for...well, for *everything*."

Danni glanced around the luxurious Sugar Beach condo where Kristine was living now. Cathedral ceilings, a built-in bar, French doors leading out to the whirlpool...it was certainly all the excess that Sugar Beach had to offer.

"So Ted is staying at the house," Danni said.

"Oh, he offered to let *me* be the one who stayed. But I needed a change."

"Kris," Danni said, "this isn't exactly a radical change. You're less than a mile from your house. You're bound to run into all your old neighbors and friends."

Kristine lifted her chin. "I've told you before. I refuse to run away. I will not give anyone that satisfaction."

Danni sank down onto a sofa so deep that her feet barely touched the floor. It was very uncomfortable. "Where did you get this monstrosity?" she muttered. "You've scarcely moved in, and already it looks like an interior decorator ran amuck in here."

"You're certainly in a cheerful mood," Kristine remarked.

"Spare me the sarcasm."

"Well," Kristine said. "I don't know why you *should* be grouchy. My life is the one falling apart. My marriage is in ruins…trying to get used to a new place…and so much else I haven't told you, Danni…."

"Do you have to be so blasted self-centered?" Danni exclaimed. "Did the thought ever occur to you that maybe you're not the only one whose life is in ruins?'' And, with that, she burst into tears.

''Oh, Danni...'' Kristine hurried over to sit beside her. She held out a tissue. ''Danni, what's wrong?'' she asked worriedly. ''It's not like you to break down like this. You're always the one who's so sensible and rational. I haven't seen you cry like this since Grandpa Daniel died.''

That only made Danni sob all the harder. Grandpa Daniel had been the one person who had truly understood her. His quiet, steady love had been a blessing for such a long time. But he was gone...and there seemed nothing left to sustain her. Nothing at all.

Kristine held the tissue in front of her, waving it as if to catch her attention. Danni grabbed it and pressed it against her eyes. The tears just wouldn't stop coming.

''Danni, you have to tell me what's wrong,'' Kristine said, her voice growing urgent. ''You're scaring me.''

''I'm pregnant.'' The words tumbled out at last. It was the very first time she had uttered them aloud, and she felt a momentary relief.

Kristine froze beside her. ''No way,'' she said, a peculiar look coming over her face.

''Yes. I'm sure. Three different home pregnancy tests can't be wrong. Not when they all say the same thing.''

''This can't be happening,'' Kristine whispered. ''It just can't.''

Danni blotted the tissue once more against her eyes. ''Do you have another one of these?''

Kristine handed her the box. ''I suppose Bryan is the father,'' she said, still in that strange manner.

''Who else could it possibly be?''

''I didn't mean to imply anything, Danni, so don't get snippy.''

''Being *snippy* is the least of my problems right now—''

''Danni. I have something to tell you, too.'' Kristine paused. ''You're not the only one who's expecting.''

Danni lifted her head and stared at her. ''Please tell me you're kidding.''

Now the tears welled in Kristine's eyes, and she took a tissue from the box. ''I'm not kidding any more than you are. I'm pregnant, all right. I've been wanting to tell you, but...everything's been so difficult. And I've hardly gotten used to the idea myself. It seems so wonderful and terrible all at once.''

Danni gave a moan. And then, because there

seemed nothing else to do, she laughed weakly through her tears. "It would be funny if it weren't so damned pathetic. Tell me that the father is Ted, Kris."

"Well, that's just the thing." Kristine spoke with elaborate care. "I'm not entirely sure who the father is. It could be Ted, or..."

"No. Don't say it. Please, just don't."

"Or Bryan."

Danni's stomach clenched, and she felt everything in the room spin. Maybe this time she really was going to faint. It had been bad enough today, trying to imagine how she would tell Bryan about the baby. But to spring *this* on him...the possibility of *two* babies...

"Tell me this isn't real, Kris. Tell me you're playing some colossal joke on me."

"I could ask the same of you, Danni."

They gazed at each other...two sisters who shared a lifetime of caring and competing.

"Truce," Danni said.

"Truce."

The words seemed to echo back through all their years. They might have once again been twelve-year-olds making up after a fight. Danni made a sound somewhere between a sob and a laugh. Kristine gave a wobbly smile.

"You know what?" she said. "I don't even have to ask. I know you haven't considered—not even for a second—*not* having the baby."

Surprised, Danni realized that was true. No matter what happened...no matter how Bryan reacted...this baby was going to be given a grand welcome.

"I know you feel the same way," Danni murmured.

Kristine put a hand to her stomach. "Oh, yes. Half the time I'm scared out of my wits. And the other half...I'm ecstatic. Does that sound crazy?"

"I just can't believe you didn't tell me, Kris. In spite of everything, how could you keep a secret like this from me?"

Kristine bit her lip. "I wanted to tell you, so much. But Danni, I just had to keep it to myself, until I could figure out what to do."

Danni felt a heaviness inside, the brief moment of camaraderie already starting to vanish. "And of course you haven't told Bryan yet."

Kristine frowned. "You make it sound like I'm deceiving him again. But I'm *not.* I just have to find the right time...."

"Maybe Ted deserves to know about it, too."

"Ted doesn't deserve anything," Kristine

snapped. ''Not after what he did. Not after the way he betrayed me.'' She stopped, as if she'd already revealed too much.

''How did he betray you?'' Danni persisted.

Kristine glanced away. ''You've already guessed. You asked me if it was another woman. The answer is...yes.''

''Who?''

''I can't do this. Don't ask me anymore.''

''Who was it?'' Danni refused to give in. There was too much at stake here.

When the words finally came, they were spoken in a wooden tone. ''One of our own neighbors. Alex Peterson. I walked in on them. That's how I found out. It was so...awful.''

Danni ached for her sister. ''What did Ted do afterward?'' she asked. She was sorry she had to put Kristine through this, but it all had to come out.

''You mean, after he zipped up his pants?'' Kristine said acidly. ''He said I was overreacting and I should calm down. He said I should let him explain.''

''If he wants you to forgive him—''

''Well, *that* would be convenient for you,'' Kristine said. ''I go back to Ted, and I'm out of the running with Bryan. Exactly what you want, isn't it?''

Danni refused to get angry. ''You probably think picking a fight with me would make you feel better. But we're going to skip it this time. You know I want you to be happy.''

Kristine propped her elbows on her knees, burying her head in her hands. ''Yes, I know that,'' she said in a muffled voice. ''But just tell me how you'd feel, Danni. Imagine you have a husband. Imagine you love him with all your heart. And imagine finding him with another woman. Could *you* forgive?''

Danni tried to picture the scenario, ''It would be horrible,'' she said. ''And honestly...I don't know if I could forgive someone who did that to me.''

''Now do you understand why I turned to Bryan?'' Kristine's voice wavered. ''Knowing I was going to see him, talk to him, *be* with him...that was the only thing that kept me going.''

Danni shook her head. ''It has to be a whole lot more complicated than that, Kris. Ted hurt you, and maybe you wanted to hurt him back—''

"Do you really think I'm that vindictive?" Kristine's voice was very quiet now.

"No, not vindictive. Just human. When you first met Bryan, you already knew about Ted's affair, didn't you?"

"Yes, I knew." Kristine stood and moved away. "That doesn't change anything, though. When the right person comes along...it's right, that's all."

Danni stood too, and faced her sister. "How can this be right," she said dully. "We're in such an impossible situation."

"I don't know, Danni. I only know that I care for Bryan. I care for him a great deal. Maybe...maybe I even love him. And I'll tell you something else. I actually hope this baby's his." She placed a hand protectively over her stomach.

Impossible situation...that was an understatement.

DANNI POSITIONED the crowbar and gave a tug. A few seconds later she heard the satisfying sound of paneling ripping loose. She couldn't understand why anyone would have put up this ugly dark stuff in the den of Bryan's house. She couldn't wait to get rid of it.

She was being careful as she worked. This morning the doctor had told her she could pursue all normal activities, within reason. That was right after he'd confirmed her pregnancy.

Danni set down the crowbar. All the wonder, all the fear came over her again. She kept feeling as if she were in a dream, and any minute she would wake up and be her old self again. Solitary, separate, no new life growing inside her.

Except that it wasn't a dream. She was going to be a mother. The word sent a shiver of apprehension through her. How could she be anybody's *mother?* That implied somebody in control, somebody who had all the answers. Not somebody who was in the middle of a colossal mess.

Danni heard a car pull up outside. She peered through the dusty window, and saw the little blue sports car. Then Bryan climbed out of the driver's seat, tie loosened, sleeves rolled up casually. He had a carefree appearance. No wonder. He didn't know yet that he had fathered a child…maybe two.

She swiveled away from the window, dropping the crowbar to the floor. This morning Bryan had sent his house key by courier to her office, and she'd taken that as tacit agreement to her plan—they would see each other as little as possible while she remodeled his house. Unfortunately, however, pregnancy had a way of altering plans. Danni had called Bryan, and asked him to meet her here. This setting was as good as any other for telling her news. The moment was almost upon her. She pictured him coming up the walk, opening the front door, walking through the house....

She heard the sound of the door, heard his footsteps. In the same protective gesture Kristine had used yesterday, Danni placed a hand over her stomach. And, a few seconds later, Bryan did appear in the den. He studied the gashes she'd made in the wall.

"You don't waste any time," he remarked, his expression bland.

"I wanted to get a head start," she said. "I'm sure your mother's going to see this place soon, and—"

"No need for her to see it." There was a quiet steeliness about him.

"I don't understand," Danni said. "I thought that was the whole idea. Remodel the house, surprise your mom."

"You can remodel all you want. It'll increase

the value of this place when I sell it. But as for the rest...I was wrong.''

Danni told herself to drop the subject. After all, she had her news to impart, and surely it was best not to waste any time getting to it. But then she remembered the night she'd met his mother, and how Elizabeth McKay had seemed so frail and valiant all at once.

''Bryan,'' Danni said, ''I disagree. Your mom really does need to see this place. She needs to know what you were thinking. Trust me.''

He glanced about restlessly. ''I already told her I bought this place. I shouldn't have said anything, though...it was a mistake. She started to remember everything about those years. The last thing she needs is to have old memories dredged up.''

''You're the one having trouble with the old memories. For your mom, it could be entirely different.''

Bryan gazed at Danni with that hard set to his face. ''It's my decision. Not something you need to be concerned about.''

The message was chillingly clear: he was shutting her out. She had no real place in his life. Everything between them so far had been a masquerade, in one form or another.

How, then, did she tell him that she was carrying his child?

Suddenly it seemed very important to break down his defenses. ''Bryan, maybe I *am* poking my nose in where it doesn't belong. But I felt a connection with your mother...as if I could understand at least a little of what she's going through. You're the most important person in her life—that's what she's feeling. And if she's going to have any peace of mind at all...the two of you have to be completely open with each other. You have to say everything that needs to be said. Before...before it's too late.'' She studied Bryan intently, trying to see if her words were having any impact at all. But his expression didn't change, not a bit. It remained unyielding.

''I'll handle things with my mother, Danni.''

He was shutting her out all right. Once again Danni put a hand to her stomach. What she felt for this new life growing inside her was overwhelming. Always the fear...but also moments of fierce, indescribable joy. She couldn't possibly share that with Bryan when his face was so hard. So implacable.

She stared at him. ''Bryan—I have something important to tell you. Something really important. But you've got to meet me halfway on this one. Can you do that—can you just be a little open, a little receptive...?''

''I'm listening,'' he said, but his expression didn't change at all. And she could tell it wasn't going to change any time soon.

She shook her head almost sorrowfully. ''I'm not going to tell you—not yet. Not while you're looking at me like that. You'll blame me, Bryan, for not telling you right away. But my news isn't going anywhere, and it just has to be different than this when I tell you. It has to be.''

She kept hoping that something in his face would soften. But it didn't happen. And so she said nothing at all.

CHAPTER TEN

ONCE AGAIN, Danni had received a phone call from Bryan's mother. And, once again, Danni hadn't been able to say no. Elizabeth McKay insisted there was something she had to do—and Danni was the one to help her do it.

It seemed no one could turn Elizabeth down. She'd also enlisted the cooperation of the nurse on duty in her apartment. Together the nurse and Danni managed to transport Elizabeth to Bryan's house. It had taken quite some doing, getting a very weak Elizabeth into Danni's car, while somehow squeezing a wheelchair into the trunk. And then, once they'd arrived at the house, getting Elizabeth into the wheelchair and pushing her up the path to the front door. Even with the nurse's help, it took considerable effort.

Elizabeth, despite her illness, treated the whole thing as a grand adventure. She even seemed to gain a bit of strength as they entered the house.

"Now, Danni, stop telling me how mad Bryan is going to be when he finds out. And stop saying *you'll* take the responsibility. The whole thing was my idea, as you very well know, and I am perfectly capable of handling my own son. Besides, as soon as he told me he'd bought this place, I knew I had to see it. Oh, how it's changed. When I worked here, it was charming. The kind of home I longed to have for Bryan and myself. Now it just seems neglected." Elizabeth stopped, struggling for breath.

"Are you all right?" Danni asked anxiously.

"Stop fussing, my dear. I want to see everything."

With the help of the nurse, Danni took Elizabeth through the place. She tried to explain her remodeling plans as succinctly as possible: the ceramic tiles instead of worn linoleum, the plaster work that would replace ugly dark paneling, the new cabinets Danni would handcraft herself, the wainscoting that would be stripped and repainted. She had to restrain herself from sharing all the details tumbling about in her mind. This house inspired her. It awoke all her imagination, all her dreams of what a home really *could* be.

At last the tour was complete, and Danni brought Elizabeth to the living room. She positioned the wheelchair next to the mantel. It was pleasingly rustic, ochre-red brick presiding over a plum-shaped hearth. This was one thing about the house she would not change at all. The fireplace would be the centerpiece of the home.

"We'll get you back as quickly as possible," Danni said, but Elizabeth gave an impatient wave.

"Danni, I told you to stop fussing. I feel like I've been sprung from jail, and I'm going to enjoy every minute of it. Sit here next to me, and tell me all about yourself and my son."

There was only a fold-out aluminum chair in a corner. Danni brought it over next to Elizabeth and sat down. The nurse disappeared diplomatically down the hall toward the kitchen, announcing that she was in search of sustenance. This left Danni and Elizabeth to themselves.

"Now, Danni. Have you and Bryan resolved your differences?"

Unaccountably, tears sprang to Danni's eyes. She turned away in dismay.

"Oh, dear," said Elizabeth. "I've done it again, haven't I? I've never been known for my tact. But I am starting to get a bit tired, and I think you'd better not make me work for any confidences. Just tell me straight out what's wrong."

The tears slid down Danni's cheeks. "There's so much you don't know," she whispered. "So much about myself I haven't told you."

"I think I can guess," Elizabeth said. "You have that special look. But why don't you tell me, dear."

Danni felt herself weaken at the gentleness in Elizabeth's voice. "I'm pregnant, Mrs. McKay," she said, then listened in horror as the words tumbled out of her mouth. How could she have confessed to Bryan's *mother,* of all people? Elizabeth would no doubt be incensed. Disillusioned, at the very least.

"My dear," said Elizabeth, her voice trembling, "I wonder if you know how happy you've just made me."

Danni stared at her through her tears. "You're not furious?"

"How on earth could I be?" Elizabeth clasped Danni's hands in both her own, her fingers thin and fragile. "To know that I will have a grandchild, to know that some small part of me will go on through you and Bryan and the family you've begun... yes, that's happiness."

Danni bent her head. "But everything's so

wrong between Bryan and me. It's all such a mess—''

''Life has a habit of getting messy,'' Elizabeth said in a wry tone. ''Sometimes Bryan has a little trouble dealing with that fact. After his father's death, he struggled so hard to get in control, and to stay there. But let me tell you something, Danni—for a while at least, having a baby means losing control of everything in your life.'' Elizabeth nodded reflectively. ''I think that might be good for Bryan. Very good, indeed.''

Danni wasn't so sure. ''If you only knew the whole story—''

''I have a feeling you've already told me the most important part. Save the rest for another time, dear.''

There was something commanding about Elizabeth despite her weakness. Some people would probably even say she was bossy.

''Ah, almost a smile,'' Elizabeth said. ''Life isn't so horrible after all, is it?''

''It's pretty awful,'' Danni admitted. ''But right now, I do feel just a little better.''

''Good. Because I'm going to feel good, and imagine you and Bryan and your family living in this house someday.''

It seemed impossible to think of creating anything with Bryan. *He* couldn't see a future for the two of them. He'd said as much. "Mrs. McKay—"

"Elizabeth."

"Elizabeth...Bryan hates this house. He would never want to live here."

Elizabeth glanced around. "What he hates is the powerlessness he felt here as a child. This house represented everything wrong with our lives back then. All the more reason, though, to transform it into a real home." She sounded so sure and matter-of-fact, as if arranging other peoples' lives was something simple, something straightforward.

Danni herself wasn't sure of anything right now. But she sat there with her hands in Elizabeth McKay's, feeling an odd sort of comfort.

She was still sitting like that when Bryan walked in. He looked from Danni to his mother, and back again. He said nothing, but he didn't need to speak. There was no mistaking the anger in his eyes.

"Hello, Bryan," his mother said regally. "Now, before you get all up in arms, I want you to know this is something I had to do. You wanted to keep me away, and that was wrong of you."

He didn't even seem to be listening. Instead, his gaze raked across Danni.

"You shouldn't have done this. She's not strong enough—"

"I am right here," Elizabeth interrupted crankily. "You don't need to talk about me like that. Talk to *me,* Bryan."

He turned back to his mother. "All right—*you're* not strong enough," he said gruffly. "This is a big mistake."

"And you're going to make sure whoever's responsible pays—that the idea?" Elizabeth said in a scoffing tone. "Well, I'm responsible. Not Danni. Not anyone else. Just me. Believe it or not, I can still make my own choices, Bryan. Would you deny me that much dignity?"

He didn't answer, but his steely expression said enough. Bryan had his own opinions, and he didn't bend for others. Not even his own mother. Suddenly Danni had had enough. There would never be a good time to tell him, no perfect moment, so she was just going to do it. She was going to have it out with him, right here and now. She stood up, opened her mouth to speak—and found Elizabeth's hand on her arm. The woman's grip was surprisingly strong.

"No, Danni," said Elizabeth in a firm voice. "This isn't the time or place."

Danni gazed at her. How well Elizabeth McKay had read her thoughts! "But he has to know, sooner or later—"

"He can wait a little while. I know how you're feeling...because I once felt the same way myself. As if I had very special, very important knowledge that could never be shared lightly."

"Hell," Bryan muttered.

"See, we're talking about you as if you weren't here," Elizabeth said loftily. "I'm sure you agree that it isn't very enjoyable. But Danni will tell you her news in her own time—when you're *ready* to hear it."

Now Danni and Bryan gazed at each other. Had he guessed what she needed to tell him? The way she and his mother had spoken surely revealed too much, and the news was probably written all over her face. But, then again...maybe he didn't want to know. Maybe that was why his own expression remained so hard and closed.

Danni felt Elizabeth's hand on her arm again. "It will be all right, my dear," Bryan's mother said softly. "You'll see."

If only Danni could believe her.

DANNI WAS TAKING a power walk on her lunch hour. She wore running shoes and a baseball cap with her linen-blend business suit. She'd heard that exercise was good for the baby, even at this early a stage. Strange how much of her life already revolved around this baby. Sometimes she desperately wanted her old life back. And other times...well, other times she couldn't imagine what her life had been like before.

"Hello, Danni."

His voice. She accelerated her pace without even thinking, and her muscles tensed as if any moment she would break into a jog. She felt torn. Did she want to run away from Bryan? Or did she want to run *to* him? Her emotions were all such a jumble!

"How did you find me?" she asked.

"A woman in your office. She was glad to give me fairly detailed directions."

Michelle, of course. Danni stole a glance at Bryan. He'd barely increased his own pace to keep step beside her. And he looked as devastatingly attractive as ever. Danni hoped their child would inherit his dark eyes....

She made a muffled sound of distress.

"What was that?" he asked.

"Nothing. You're obviously here for a reason, Bryan. What is it?"

"Maybe I wanted to apologize," he said in that gruff tone of his. "For yesterday...for coming down on you hard, when my mother was the one who put you up to it."

"Some apology," Danni muttered. "You make your mother and me sound like accomplices in a caper." She drew a deep breath. "Your mom may be sick, but she's still an adult, Bryan. She needed to see that place. She needed to remember all the things you want to forget. She's looking back over her life...taking stock of the past, trying to arrange the future. I admire her courage—"

"It took way too much out of her. She's landed in the hospital again." His voice was carefully expressionless, but when Danni looked at him she saw the pain in his eyes. She stopped abruptly.

"Oh, Bryan, I'm so sorry. I didn't mean...I didn't want to hurt her in any way. I wanted to help...."

"I did ask you to stay out of it, Danni."

Oh, yes, he'd made every effort to shut her out of his life. "How's Elizabeth doing?" Danni asked after a strained pause.

"As well as can be expected," Bryan said. "Ordering the doctors and nurses around. Insisting she knows better than everybody else."

They'd reached the waterfront. Feeling a tightness in her throat, Danni crossed the street and went to walk along the bay. An ancient schooner rocked at its moorings as workmen hammered on deck. Restoring something old, something worth saving...

Bryan continued to walk beside her. "Believe it or not, I didn't come here to accuse you—to make you feel bad," he said.

"Why *did* you come?"

"Hell if I know," he said in a low voice.

Now was her opportunity to tell him. *Bryan, I'm carrying your child. And so, it seems, is my sister Kristine.*

She made another despairing sound.

"Are you all right, Danni?" He spoke cautiously. Maybe he did suspect her news...maybe not. But she still got the very distinct impression he didn't want to hear it.

Wait until he heard the part about Kristine.

The pungent ocean air drifted over Danni. It made her stomach churn just a bit. The oddest things affected her nowadays.

"I'm fine," she said, as if to convince herself. "Just fine." She stopped and propped her elbows against a low wall, gazing out over the bay. Bryan stopped beside her.

"I'm so very sorry about your mother," she said, her voice low. "It's hard to explain, but...I feel comfortable around her. Almost like I used to feel around Grandpa Daniel. As if your mother...accepts me. No questions asked."

"She talks about you a lot," Bryan said after a moment. "She keeps saying how glad she is that she met you."

Tears were always too near the surface for Danni lately. Maybe that was another part of pregnancy. Danni blinked rapidly, but the tears spilled anyway.

"Hell," Bryan said, and he handed her a handkerchief.

She took it, blotting her eyes. "I'm surprised," she said in a wobbly voice. "A man who carries a handkerchief. That's kind of old-fashioned, isn't it?"

"Apparently my dad used to carry them," he said grudgingly.

So...Bryan showed his feelings in unspoken ways. Perpetuating a small tradition of his father's—that was an expression of emotion, all right. Except that Bryan would probably never admit it.

"Please tell your mother how sorry I am that she's in the hospital," Danni said. "Please tell her—"

"Aren't you going to go see her yourself?" Bryan asked.

"According to you, I've done enough damage already."

"She's...asking for you," Bryan said.

Danni pressed the handkerchief to her face again. It smelled clean and fresh, and it was made of the finest cotton.

"I wish you could have heard yourself just now," she murmured. "The reluctance in your voice. You hated telling me that your mother wants to see me. Because...in some small measure...that means letting me into your life."

"Danni—"

"Look, if you want me to, I'll go see your mom right now," Danni said. "I'll just stop by the office and tell them they have to do without me a little while longer. You can come with me—or not." Feeling a welcome surge of energy, she went striding off in her running shoes.

When, after a moment, she glanced back at Bryan, she had the satisfaction of seeing that he looked decidedly unsettled.

And this time he did have to hurry to catch up with her.

DANNI SAT BESIDE Elizabeth McKay's hospital bed, clasping the woman's frail hand in her own. Bryan had driven her here, but had been asked to leave immediately afterward. Elizabeth had insisted that he go check on the cats, just to make sure no feline mishaps had occurred. Danni suspected that what Elizabeth really wanted was to get him out of the room so the two of them could have a heart-to-heart.

Danni smiled in spite of herself, but then she studied Elizabeth in concern. "I'm awfully sorry I landed you back in this place."

"You're blaming yourself? How self-destructive of you," Elizabeth chided. "Especially when the whole thing was my own doing. Listen, dear...even *I* knew that eventually I'd be back here. Stop wallowing in guilt."

There was something very refreshing about the way Elizabeth dispensed with niceties.

"All right," Danni said. "The truth is, I'm glad you saw the house. I'm glad you know

Bryan bought it for you. He could probably never come right out and tell you he loves you...but the house shows it.''

''Goodness, his father was just the same that way. Heaven forbid Randall should betray any sentiment. Except, when I least expected it, he'd show up with the most extravagant bouquet. Flowers we couldn't afford...'' Elizabeth's face softened, and her eyelids drifted downward. Clearly she was lost in the past. Danni just sat quietly as she held Elizabeth's hand.

After a long while, Elizabeth opened her eyes again. ''Still here, Danni?''

''If you want me to leave, I'll go.''

''You know perfectly well I don't want you to go,'' Elizabeth said with a show of spirit. ''Now, out with it. You haven't told him yet, have you?''

Shame washed over Danni. ''No. I've been a coward.''

''Nonsense. You've been a woman guarding a beautiful secret. You're afraid that telling Bryan might actually ruin it. Men never react the way we want them to with these things. When I told Randall *he* was going to be a father, he went out and got drunk. Which, believe it or not, was quite unusual for him. He had many faults, but imbibing was not one of them."

This time Danni gave a real smile. "And then what happened?"

"Well, he had a dreadful hangover, and it took him two days to recover. And then he went out and bought a bicycle for his future child. The most expensive two-wheeler he could find—and I was barely a month pregnant."

"It sounds," said Danni, "as if you loved your husband very much."

"That I did," Elizabeth murmured. "He drove me crazy...and I was crazy about him at the same time. After he died...people hardly waited a decent interval before telling me I should marry again." Elizabeth spoke scornfully. "I don't know why they thought it was any of *their* business. But I always knew that Randy was the only one for me. Knew it the first minute I saw him. And if I had any consolation after he died...it was the fact that he'd left me with a piece of him. A son. That's the way it is, Danni. You love someone, and you crave making a child together. You want something of your love to live beyond you."

Those blasted tears came again. Danni felt like a leaky faucet. She groped in her pocket for

Bryan's handkerchief, and really started weeping. "I'm sorry," she said in a soggy voice.

"Will you please stop apologizing?" Elizabeth asked testily. "Have a cry. It'll be good for you."

"It's all I've been doing lately."

"Cry as much as you need to. And take care of yourself, Danni. Take care of my grandchild, too. Wait to tell Bryan...but don't wait too long."

"Elizabeth, there's still so much you don't know. So much you have a right to know—"

"I know the only thing that matters. You love Bryan, and you're going to have his child. You *do* love my son, don't you?"

"Yes," Danni uttered miserably. "It's just like you said. He drives me crazy...but I'm crazy about him, too."

Now Elizabeth patted Danni's hand. "I thought as much. Yesterday, when you gave in to me and took me to see the house...I figured you wouldn't do something like that unless you cared about Bryan very much. You cared enough to go against him."

"That doesn't make a whole lot of sense," Danni said.

"Yes, it does. If you love someone—when

you know what's best for him, you go right ahead and do it. And showing me the house...that was best for Bryan.''

''I thought I was doing it for you,'' Danni said quietly.

''You were doing it for both of us. Somehow Bryan and I have to come to terms about our past. About Randall, really. Because, in a strange way, that house represents Bryan's father. I wouldn't have worked there if he'd been a better provider...so Bryan takes out his resentment on the place. Risky stuff. He buys the house to show that he got the better of it—but now it's confronting him every day.''

''He keeps acting like he wants to turn around and sell it,'' Danni said.

''Don't let that happen,'' Elizabeth instructed. ''At least, not until Bryan has resolved his feelings about his father.'' Her voice was growing strained, as if every word cost her more and more effort.

''You should rest now,'' Danni said, glancing toward the door. ''I'm surprised one of the nurses hasn't come in to tell us as much.''

''They're leaving us alone on purpose. They know people on their deathbeds need to get everything said.''

Danni's fingers tightened involuntarily around Elizabeth's. "Don't say that," she said. "I don't want...I don't want you to go." More tears pricked behind her eyelids.

"If you want to know the truth, Danni—myself, I'm torn. I'm so anxious to see Randall again I scarcely know what to do. But I want to stay here, too. I want to watch my son grow older...I want to know *you* better...something tells me you'd be the daughter I always wanted...and I want to see my grandchildren. I don't expect you and Bryan to stop at just one...."

The irony of that was too much for Danni. She put her head down on the bed as those endless tears trickled out. And she felt Elizabeth's hand gently smoothing her hair.

"I think I will rest now after all, Danni. You know something? Those deathbed scenes in the movies are all nonsense. Nobody goes that easily, that conveniently. Something tells me I'm going to be here for a while yet. So you leave, and I'll take a little nap."

Danni stood shakily. She leaned over and kissed Elizabeth's cheek. "I love you," she said. "I hardly know you, but I do love you."

"I feel the same. I love you, my dear daughter-in-law. Because that's what I want you to be...."

Danni turned and walked quickly from the room, before the tears truly engulfed her.

CHAPTER ELEVEN

THE SHADOWS of evening gathered in Elizabeth's hospital room. Bryan stood at the window, watching the sun set in a glory of rose and vermilion. The processes of nature were relentless. The sun came up, went down regardless of human turmoil. He supposed that was comforting in a way.

His mother's breathing was labored, the rhythm erratic. He felt himself tense with each inhale and exhale of air. She'd been sleeping most of the afternoon since Danni had left. But it was not a restful sleep. Her head moved now and then on the pillow, and her breath seemed to cost her. Bryan just wanted her to rest. He wanted her to have some comfort, some ease.

Outside in the corridor, footsteps went by now and then. And, now and then, he heard talk and laughter. Other lives went on unheeding, even as one life wound down.

He went to sit down beside his mother's bed.

He'd brought papers from the office—financial statements, projections for the San Diego-Tijuana venture. Robert and the other architects were starting to worry they wouldn't be able to pull in enough investors to get the project off the ground. Bryan was concerned about that, too. But right now he couldn't think about it. His own life was reduced to this hospital room, to the sound of life ebbing away. His mother's life.

"Bryan," she said quite clearly, opening her eyes, "have you had any dinner yet?"

He gave the faintest of smiles. She was going to play out her part as his mother, right up until the end. "Not yet," he said.

"What's the matter with you? Go down to the cafeteria, get something to eat. I'm not going anywhere. And I refuse to lie here and listen to your stomach growling."

"It's not growling."

"It *will* be. Go eat something so I don't have to worry."

Danni complained about him always needing to be in control. Maybe he'd gotten that trait from his mother. Even now she was trying to orchestrate all the little details.

"*Go,* Bryan."

He went—not because he was hungry, but because he wanted her to have whatever small satisfactions she could. He walked down one hallway, then another. This hospital was a maze, but already he knew it well.

He arrived at the cafeteria, and automatically made a few selections. He sat down, tried to eat. Right now, however, that seemed like one more pointless activity. At last he deposited his tray and went back upstairs. Apprehension clenched his insides. Maybe he shouldn't have left—

But his mother was wide-awake. "What did you have?" she asked.

He tried to humor her. "A couple of rolls. Something you'd call a green-bean casserole, I guess. It wasn't bad."

"I'm sure it was absolutely dreadful. What else?"

"A piece of chocolate cake," he told her. "That was good."

"I hope so." She sighed, seeming to sink back farther into the pillows. "Now, Bryan, let's get this over with. My parting wishes and so forth."

"Let's not," Bryan said.

She gave him a stern look. "First and foremost," she said, "I don't want you to be stupid about Danni."

"Don't know exactly what you mean," he said.

"Yes, you do. There is no question that Danni's the woman you should marry—but you're just dense enough not to see it."

"I like Danni, but—"

"Just listen to yourself," Elizabeth scoffed. "You 'like' her. You couldn't possibly admit that you spend every waking hour thinking about her."

"That, too," he said.

His mother shook her head against the pillows. "You really are impossible, Bryan. But just listen to this. If you don't give Danni what she needs from you…if you don't love her with all your heart and more…I will *haunt* you. Do you understand?"

His mother was so strong-willed, he believed her entirely capable of haunting anybody. Just his luck that he was the most likely candidate.

"Got it," he said.

"I certainly hope so." She closed her eyes. "And about the house you bought for me. It needs to be your house, not mine, and you need to stop blaming it for all your father's shortcomings. Come to think of it, you need to stop blaming your dad. I never helped you very much with that, did I? Because I blamed him too...for leaving us....''

After a moment she stirred again. ''I'd like you to live in the house, Bryan. With Danni. And with all three of my cats...now I think I'll rest just a little more.''

Long into the night she slept. Eventually her breathing slowed, grew more difficult. Bryan listened, unable to stir from the room, unable to face his conviction that she would not wake again. And somewhere in that endless night a memory came to him, unbidden. He'd been about eight or nine maybe, priding himself on his self-sufficiency. Except that his mother had been very late in coming home, and he'd started to get scared. He'd imagined her dying somewhere, just like his dad. Leaving him. Uneasiness had turned to fear, and all he'd wanted was for her to come through the front door and make one of her wisecracks.

At last she'd appeared, and his relief had been a physical thing. He'd run to her and given her an uncustomary hug. She'd hugged him back, holding him tightly. Only much later did he learn that she'd been out cleaning one of her houses that day—clear across town—and her old car had broken down on the way home.

Now all he wanted was for her to open her eyes, and make one of her wisecracks. But Elizabeth McKay slept on.

KRISTINE HAD A mean backhand. She smacked the ball over the net so forcefully that Danni didn't have a chance. Danni trailed after the ball, picked it up and gave it an unenthusiastic tap with her racket. This time it barely made the journey over to Kristine's side. Kristine jogged up to the net.

"Could you please put a little more effort into this?" she asked in a low, intent voice. "Everybody's *watching*."

Danni glanced around. "I don't see anybody looking at us."

"Not *overtly*. They know how to be subtle in this place. But, believe me, they're making note of everything we do."

The Sugar Beach Country Club courts were beautifully apportioned. The members were beautifully apportioned, too. And Danni felt she'd had quite enough of both.

"Kris, we really do need to talk."

"My serve," called Kristine, and the ball came sailing over again. Kristine looked very fashionable in her knit top, swirly tennis skirt, pristine white headband, and equally pristine wristbands. Danni wore gym shorts and a T-shirt—and Kristine almost hadn't allowed her on the court.

"Who do you think we're fooling?" Danni asked now.

Kristine glared at her. "Could you cooperate at least a little?"

Danni relented, and they finished the set. It was a relief afterward to go sit at one of the patio tables and order iced tea.

"Actually," Danni said, "I've changed my mind. I'll just have a glass of milk."

Kristine paused. "Make that two milks," she told the waiter. When he'd gone, she shook her head. "I can just imagine what everyone will have to say about *that.* You and me *both* drinking milk in the middle of the day."

"Now you're getting paranoid," Danni told her. "I can't believe your friends are going to sneak into the kitchen to see what you ordered."

"The waiter will talk," Kristine said ominously.

"Kris, you're being ridiculous."

Kristine sighed. "You just don't get it, do you, Danni? At Sugar Beach, people are constantly posturing with each other. The only way they can reassure themselves that they're still on top is to make sure someone's at the bottom. And, right now…I'm sinking to the bottom."

"So why," asked Danni in exasperation, "do you put up with this place? Why not just leave?" She glared at her sister. "I know, I know—you don't want to give them the satisfaction."

Danni shook her head and leaned back in her cushioned chair. The umbrella overhead was tilted at just the right angle. It allowed just a little bit of sun, but not too much. They thought of everything at Sugar Beach Country Club. If you were being scrutinized by everyone here, at least you could do it in luxury and comfort.

Danni wished the comfort could extend to her soul. She wished the same for Kristine, too. She studied her sister—the misery on Kristine's face had deepened so that not even her dark glasses could provide sufficient disguise.

"Kris…something else has happened, hasn't it? I wish you'd talk about it."

"How could things possibly have gotten any worse than before?" Kristine muttered.

"Apparently they have."

Kristine sighed. "You know what, Danni? You really are the person who knows me best in the whole world.'' She lowered her voice. ''All right, I'll tell you what happened. Yesterday *she* came to see me.''

''You mean—''

''Shush. Not so loud. Alex Peterson,'' Kris said sotto voce. ''My *former* friend and neighbor. She said we ought to have a talk to clear the air. I said nothing doing. She said she loved Ted, and he loved *her*. I said get the hell out.'' Kristine took a shaky breath. ''Danni, it was awful. After Ted had sworn to me that it didn't mean anything, and that it was over. How am I ever supposed to believe anything he says again?''

Danni didn't have an answer for that. The two glasses of milk arrived, tall and frosty. Kristine waited until the waiter was out of hearing range.

''So you see how it is,'' she said at last. ''There really is no hope for Ted and me. Bryan...Bryan is all I have.''

Danni gazed incredulously at her sister. ''Do you honestly think Bryan is still a possibility at this point?''

''Why not?'' Kristine said in a defiant tone. ''He can't ignore the fact that...well...'' Her voice dropped even lower. ''He can't ignore the fact that he's started a *family*.''

''And then some.'' Danni wanted to laugh, but she felt too tired. Another symptom of pregnancy, as well as stress and worry: an overwhelming sleepiness that assaulted her at the most inopportune moments. ''Kris,'' she said after a moment, ''you can't ignore the possibility that your baby—''

''Shh!''

''That your baby may be Ted's,'' Danni persisted. ''He deserves to know as much.''

''No, he doesn't.''

Danni tried again. ''Well, Bryan deserves to know.''

''Have *you* told him?'' Kristine asked.

''No, I haven't. And neither have you, obviously. So,'' Danni said firmly, ''we're going to tell him together. I don't care if we have to camp out on his doorstep. We'll take strength in numbers.''

''Way too many numbers,'' Kristine said sardonically.

Danni felt another spark of exasperation. ''Okay, so it's going to be a big shock. But he did have a little something to do with it.''

Kristine glanced away in a very suspicious manner.

"Kris," Danni said with a feeling of dread. "What is it you're not telling me this time?"

"Nothing."

"Out with it," Danni said.

"I suppose you'll find out sooner or later. It's just that...when Bryan and I...well, I told him birth control was all taken care of. I told him...I was on the pill."

Danni felt sick inside. "I don't believe it," she whispered. "Another lie. And then when he and I...he obviously assumed..."

"I'm sorry." Kristine said.

Now Danni was at a loss for words.

"Danni," Kristine said, her voice suddenly sad. "Please don't look at me like that. As if you...hate me."

Of course she could never hate her sister. It would never come to that. But right now she didn't like Kristine very much.

She stood, leaving the shade and comfort of the umbrella. "Come on, Kris. We're not going to make this any worse than it already is. We're going to tell Bryan—and we're going to do it now."

IT SEEMED Danni and Kristine really might have to camp out on Bryan's doorstep. They'd been parked in front of his apartment for a full two hours, waiting for him to arrive home from work. They were still surrounded by luxury, sitting as they did in Kristine's Mercedes, but that didn't make the task ahead seem any more pleasant.

"We all live in little boxes," Kristine said lugubriously. "Bryan in his apartment, you in yours, and now me in that ridiculous condo."

"Your condo isn't exactly a little box," Danni reminded her in a dry tone.

"You know what I mean. In spite of everything that's happened, we're all so separate."

That much was very true. Right now Danni felt like the loneliest person in the world.

At last the blue sports car drove up. Bryan got out, and instantly Danni knew something was wrong. She saw it in the way he walked. Usually he had such a forceful stride. But now…now he walked as if he could hardly bear to take another step.

Kristine must have seen it too, for she was out of the Mercedes in a flash and hurrying up to Bryan.

"What is it, Bryan?" she asked anxiously. Danni reached her side just as Bryan spoke. His voice was utterly weary.

"My mother died this afternoon."

"Oh, no," Danni murmured, her own voice clotting with tears. Yesterday, when she'd visited Elizabeth in the hospital, she'd known full well that the end was near. But her body still recoiled in shock, still tensed at the unfairness of it all. Because Elizabeth *shouldn't* have died. She had been so full of life and vigor despite the ravages of her illness. No, it wasn't fair.

It seemed all Danni could do was stand there, the tears streaming down her face once again. But Kristine stepped closer to Bryan and put her arms around him.

"I'm sorry," she said. "So very sorry."

He did not seem to welcome Kristine's embrace, but he didn't move away from it, either. Seeing the two of them together, her sister and Bryan, sent a knife of envy and pain through Danni. And then she felt ashamed. How could she be experiencing something as petty as jealousy when she had just learned of Elizabeth's death?

Danni continued to stand as if frozen, caught in the ferment of her own emotions. But suddenly Kristine was all efficiency, seeming to know exactly what to do. She led Bryan up to his door, got him inside the apartment, prodded him over to his couch.

"Lie down," she commanded. "You're exhausted. Danni and I will take care of details." She slipped off his shoes, made sure he was stretched out. He didn't argue. He closed his eyes, sorrow and suffering imprinted on his features. Danni ached for him, but it was Kristine who continued to know exactly what to do. She led Danni into the kitchen.

"We need to fix something for him to eat," she said, opening the refrigerator. "And don't assume that just because I had a maid for four years that I don't know how to cook." There was something reassuring about Kristine's brisk tone. Danni sat down and watched as her sister made a pastrami and provolone sandwich.

"It figures," Danni said. "Bryan would never have ordinary bologna and cheese in his fridge."

"Of course not," Kristine said. "Neither would I." She tiptoed out to the living room, then tiptoed back again. "He's asleep," she said. "Let's hope he's out for a while. He needs it. There'll be time enough to deal with everything else later."

"You're being so capable," Danni remarked.

"Don't make it sound like such a novelty,"

Kristine said with a touch of asperity. "I do have a few surprises in me. Just because you're usually the competent one..."

Danni propped her elbows on the table. "I can't believe she's gone. I just can't."

"I never met her," Kristine said. "I wish I had."

"I only saw her three times," Danni said reflectively. "Yet somehow I feel as if I'd known her for a very long while."

"Three times," Kristine said. "I didn't know you'd met her at all."

"For goodness' sake," Danni muttered. "Let's not quibble about *this,* too."

Kristine held her hand up. "All right, all right. This obviously isn't the time or place."

Odd...Elizabeth herself had used those exact same words. *Not the time or place to tell Bryan he's a father...*

"I told her, Kris. I told her about...the baby. I wanted to tell her the rest of it, too. The part about there being, for all intents and purposes, *two* Dannis—"

"One Kris and one Danni," Kristine said emphatically.

"Right. But whenever I tried to tell her, she

stopped me. She said knowing about the baby was enough. It made her so happy.''

''It did?'' Kristine asked wistfully. ''I'm glad she felt that way. Because...because Bryan certainly won't be happy, when we tell him. Which of course we can't right now. He has enough to cope with at the moment.''

''Yes, he does.'' Anxiety clenched at Danni. She'd been so ready to have it over, done with. But now they would have to wait, and she wondered if she could endure it.

Kristine went to peer in the living room again. ''Very much asleep,'' she announced when she came back. ''We may as well share this sandwich, Danni. When he wakes up, I'll make him another.''

Danni wasn't hungry, but she knew she had to make an effort to eat properly. She took her half of the sandwich. Then she glanced around the kitchen, studying all the chrome and porcelain and hand-fired tile. The place would have been too perfect, if not for a few dirty dishes in the sink.

''Bryan doesn't have a real home,'' she said.

''Not yet,'' said Kristine.

''You think you're the one who can make a home for him.''

"Why not?" Kris asked. "If I know anything about Bryan, he believes in taking care of his responsibilities."

Impossible. Everything is so impossible.

"I wouldn't want Bryan to stay with me just because of responsibility," Danni said. "You wouldn't want it, either."

Kristine stared down at her plate, an odd hardness to her face. "I don't think you know what I want, Danni."

Indeed, Danni wondered if she knew her sister at all anymore.

CHAPTER TWELVE

BRYAN WOKE to nighttime. He sat up groggily, rubbing his head, forgetting for a moment what had happened. He told himself he had to get to the hospital, see how his mother was doing—

She had died. There was nowhere he needed to go. A heavy dullness settled upon him.

Someone clicked on a lamp across the room. Soft light spilled upon a vision coming toward him. Danni, beautiful in white. Tennis whites, to be exact.

"You're still here, Danni?"

"Kris," she said, her voice a bit sharp.

Lord, he couldn't believe he could still make that mistake. At the moment, though, it didn't seem to matter a whole lot. Nothing seemed to matter.

Danni came to stand beside her sister. The real Danni this time. "How are you feeling?" she asked.

"Not much of anything."

Kristine held out a plate with a sandwich on it. "You need to eat," she said. "Even if you don't feel like it."

He took the sandwich, and automatically took a bite. "I have phone calls to make," he said. "Her friends in Saint Louis. A cousin in Oregon—"

"I'll do it," Kristine said. "Just tell me where the numbers are."

He didn't have the energy to argue, and directed her to the address book in a desk drawer. A few minutes later, she was seated at the desk, her tone muted as she began communicating the news. Meanwhile, Danni hovered uncertainly.

"Something to drink, Bryan?" she asked with a forced formality. Maybe death did that. It was like another presence in the room, making you want to whisper and give it a wide berth.

"I think I need a beer," he said.

She brought a bottle and a glass from the kitchen, even started pouring for him.

"You don't have to wait on me," he said. "You shouldn't even be here."

"We'll leave," she said instantly. "You probably want some time to yourself."

"No," he said, surprising himself. "Don't go."

Half an hour later, the situation seemed definitely surreal: two beautiful blondes organizing his life.

"I'm sorry to bring this up," Kristine said, "but the funeral arrangements..."

He hadn't even thought about that. "My mother never said what she wanted. I guess in these cases you just look in the phone book."

"Not at all," said Kristine, taking charge yet again. "We're going to give her a proper send-off. I'll call my caterer, and—"

"Kris," Danni said. "This isn't a debutante ball, for crying out loud."

"Well, why shouldn't it be an occasion? I bet Elizabeth would have liked a little fanfare. It probably would have made her smile."

"Yeah," said Bryan. "I think it would."

Danni grew quiet. And then she gave a nod. "Yes, Kris is right. It would make Elizabeth happy."

It got even more surreal after that, Kristine sitting there with a notepad and pencil, jotting down plans. "Petit fours and truffle cake for the reception."

"Please," said Danni. "Don't call it a reception."

"Well, a wake then, if that makes you feel

better. And I can book a very good string quartet. What kind of music did your mother like, Bryan?''

''Country, from about fifty years ago.''

''Hmm.'' Kristine tapped the pencil against her mouth. ''That will be a bit of a challenge, but I'll see what I can do. As far as the guest list…I'll make sure her Saint Louis friends have plenty of notice to fly in. Cars to pick them up at the airport, of course…''

In a bizarre way, it was all making him feel better. He sat back on the couch, thinking what a kick Elizabeth would have gotten out of this. He wondered what she would have said if she'd known about both Kristine and Danni. He could almost hear her voice.

An embarrassment of riches, son. You've really got yourself into a fix now.

''The one thing we haven't discussed is the eulogy,'' Kristine said in a gentle tone. ''You're the one who has to deliver it, Bryan.''

''I don't think so.''

''Nothing too formal,'' she added, as if she hadn't heard him. ''You know what's best? Just to get up there and remember things about your mother. And, after you're done, anyone else who wants to can get up and talk about her. A gathering of friends, reminiscing. Sort of like a coffee klatch, you know.''

He almost smiled at that. Elizabeth had never been one for coffee klatches.

''I think that just about wraps it up.'' Kristine stood, snapping shut her little notebook and returning it to her purse. ''Danni and I are going to take off now, let you get some real sleep.'' She knew exactly how long to stay, and when to leave. She was a whiz at etiquette—probably should have been a social director, Bryan thought.

Danni, meanwhile, had been uncharacteristically subdued, like a kid staying next to the wall at a school dance. Yet her quietude was something of a relief after Kristine's nonstop master planning.

''See you tomorrow, Bryan,'' she said simply. ''Thanks for everything you did tonight.''

''Kristine did all the work. She's amazing, you know,'' Danni told him. He guessed that was part of being a twin. The perpetual loyalty. Suddenly he wondered what it would be like to have a sibling to share this with him. A sister, or a brother. It was an experience completely foreign to him, hard to imagine. But maybe it would have taken away some of the loneliness.

Danni and Kristine left, and he was alone in his apartment. He wandered around, feeling at a loss. It didn't seem right to do any of the normal things. Go through the mail, check out the ten o'clock news, brush his teeth.

He sat down again, leaning his head back against the couch. When he closed his eyes, images flickered in his mind like old home movies. A vague memory of his father laughing at one of his own jokes. His mother, an Easter hat perched precariously atop her head. His mother again, reading aloud to him when he was a kid, reading from the books she herself had loved as a child…

He slept, but even his dreams gave him no peace. Danni and Kristine seemed to dance through them. And, in his dreams, he kept getting them mixed up. It disturbed him, and he tried to fix it, but the solution eluded him. Then both of them faded altogether, and even in his dreams he was alone.

ELIZABETH MCKAY'S funeral turned out to be a beautiful farewell. Sunlight streamed in through the stained-glass windows of the church, sending beams of ruby and gold and turquoise over the pews. The string quartet provided by Kristine was just the right touch. And Bryan, for all his reluctance to speak, delivered a eulogy that had his audience smiling through their tears. He told little stories about Elizabeth that brought her touchingly to life. Afterward her friends stood too, sharing their own stories. The quartet played again, bringing the event to a fitting finale.

Then a row of cars departed for the cemetery. The graveside ceremony was heartfelt, more tears shed, more memories shared. Some time later the mourners returned to the church.

The chapel grounds provided a serene setting for the gathering Kristine had orchestrated. Buffet tables had been set up under a grape arbor. The guests wandered along the hedges and among the flower and herb gardens. And somehow Kristine had obtained old records of the country ballads Elizabeth had loved. They played in the background, again seeming to bring her to life. Bryan, through it all, observed an unnatural restraint, a too rigid control. Danni wished he could let go a little. How would he ever truly grieve if he kept his emotions locked up so tightly?

And then there was Kristine, who was having a hard time keeping her emotions under control. She took an unexpected call on her cell phone, then disappeared for a long while. When she returned, she wore her dark glasses—definitely a bad sign.

Danni took her aside. "What's wrong now?" she asked apprehensively.

"Plenty," Kristine muttered. "Can you believe Ted actually had the nerve to call me?"

"What did he want?" Danni asked, her sense of apprehension only growing.

"He wanted...he wanted to know if I'd seen his engraved silver cuff links!"

Danni considered. "Well, I think that's promising, don't you? If I remember, you gave him a pair of engraved cuff links on your anniversary...what was it, two years ago? It sounds like he's trying to evoke a pleasant memory of the two of you—"

"Danni, just *stop*. Ted doesn't deserve to be psychoanalyzed. And I told him before I moved out, that I'd thrown away the damn cuff links!" Kristine's voice rose precipitously. Always so concerned about not causing a scene, she was about to create a major one now. Danni took hold of her arm and dragged her into the chapel, the only privacy available.

"Okay, calm down," she instructed her sister.

"How can anybody be calm?" Kristine paced

up and down the aisle. ''I told him I never wanted to speak to him again...yet he thinks he can call me up, just like that...and I'll melt and go crawling back to him.''

''I'm sure,'' said Danni, ''he doesn't expect any crawling. As for the melting—you could at least give him a chance to tell *his* side of the story.''

''Ha. I already know his side. He jumped into bed with Alex Peterson the first chance he got.''

This all seemed rather a volatile subject for the hushed atmosphere of the church. Nonetheless, you had to work with what you had. Danni prodded Kristine to sit down in one of the pews.

''This place makes a person reflect a little,'' Danni said. ''For instance, right now I'm wondering exactly why Ted had an affair.''

Kristine frowned. ''Who cares about whys and wherefores. He did it, that's all.''

''Just like you had an affair with Bryan...for no apparent reason.''

Kristine clenched her hands in her lap and stared down at them. ''It's not the same thing.''

''Maybe not,'' Danni admitted. ''But you would never have looked at Bryan if Ted hadn't betrayed you.''

Kristine was silent for a long moment. ''Are

you trying to say that Ted cheated on me because he felt our marriage was unhappy... unfulfilling? Because if that *is* what you're trying to say, it's just not true. *I* was happy. *I* was fulfilled."

"Was Ted happy, though." Danni made it a statement, not a question. Kristine glared at her from behind the dark glasses.

"This is really low of you, Danni. How rotten do you want me to feel? And I know you're only saying all this so you can try to get me out of the way, and have a clear shot at Bryan."

Danni battled a familiar frustration. "How many times do I have to tell you—neither one of us has any hope of a future with Bryan. This isn't about him. It's about you and Ted...and about me, trying to help."

"Help like this I don't need," muttered Kristine. She sprang up as if she could not bear to sit still. Once again she paced the aisle between the pews. "I wish I *had* thrown out his lousy cuff links. Why I ever had them engraved is beyond me—"

"I remember the engraving," Danni said. "The initials T and K, joined in a lovers' knot."

"Well, the knot unraveled, didn't it? Everything's over.'' She gave a mournful finality to those last two words, and Danni fought it.

''Why not give him a chance to talk to you, at least—''

''No chances,'' said Kristine. ''He's probably still spending his nights with *her.*'' She slipped off her glasses. Her eyes were red-rimmed, but there was a hardness to them. ''I told him everything just now, Danni. I told him that I'd had my *own* affair. I told him I was madly in love with Bryan. And I told him I was going to have Bryan's child. Oh, that part really got to him. Not too long ago he was making noises about starting a family. I've started one, all right...without him.''

Kristine spoke so coldly, so bitterly. It sent an iciness through Danni. ''You're lying to him. The baby *could* be his.''

''He'll never know that. After what he's done to me...he'll never know. But Bryan—that's a different story.'' Kristine began marching out of the chapel. Danni hurried after her, the feeling of dread inside her only mushrooming.

''Kris! What are you doing—''

''I'm going to do what we should have all along. Tell Bryan the truth.''

''Kris,'' Danni said, her voice low and urgent.

"Not here. Not now. He already has enough to handle."

Kristine strode along almost exuberantly. "It's what you wanted, Danni. Let's get it out there. Let's kick it around." She reached Bryan, who was standing a little apart. Danni could only watch with a mounting sense of horror.

"Bryan," Kris said in a clear, forceful voice. "Danni's pregnant. So am I. And you're the father."

ALL THE GUESTS had departed, but the remnants of the gathering remained. The buffet tables under the arbor, still half-laden with food. The doors of the church, still open. A dark limousine, still parked at the curb…it was melancholy. The funeral over, but nothing settled. Nothing resolved.

Bryan sat in one of the chairs that had been placed in the grass. He looked from Danni to Kristine, and then back again. He didn't say a word, but his face was expressive enough. It revealed shock, disbelief…dismay.

"I thought maybe you'd suspected," Danni said. "About me, at least."

He ran a hand through his hair, rumpling it.

"Maybe I did," he said reluctantly. "You kept talking about important news. But two..."

Apparently he couldn't even finish the sentence. *Two babies.*

Kristine, through all of this, looked frightened—as if she'd jumped in too deep, only to discover she couldn't swim. "It is rather overwhelming, isn't it?" she asked in a small voice. "What are we going to do?"

Bryan gazed at her...and the steeliness in his eyes was back full force. The anger, too. Because everything had come out—including the fact that Kristine had lied about birth control.

"We're going to handle it," Danni said, suddenly brisk and in charge.

"How?" Kristine asked, still in that uncertain voice.

"We just will—that's all. We'll work it out somehow. I can raise a child perfectly well on my own. And so can you, for that matter. Since Bryan did not voluntarily enter into this arrangement, he's hardly liable—"

"You sound like a damn lawyer," Bryan said. "I'm part of this, whether I like it or not. And...I'll handle it."

"How?" Kristine asked again.

That was the big question of the day.

DANNI HAD NEVER seen so many rocking horses in her life. They filled an entire floor in the Hobbyhorse Toys factory building. Rows and rows of them—carved, painted, decked out with bows and tinsel. They made Danni's head swim.

"Guess we got a good response to the contest," Larry remarked.

"No kidding," Danni said. As she picked her way through the thicket of horses, she told herself she should be grateful. Her idea had been a great success. But somehow she took no pleasure in the knowledge. All she could think about was the expression on Bryan's face when he'd learned he was going to be a father. Twice over.

Danni had jumped in to explain that it might not be twice over. That hadn't seemed to moderate the shock, however. He and Danni and Kristine had reached no conclusion…none at all.

Danni gripped the clipboard she was carrying. She needed to be focusing on work. The Hobbyhorse executives had decided to move up the announcement of the competition results to allow for additional publicity before Christmas. That meant Danni and her team had only forty-eight hours to select a winner.

"This one's kind of cute," said Michelle,

stopping in front of a rocking horse painted all over with spots.

"It looks like a dalmatian, not a horse," Danni said. "Cross it off the list."

"That's harsh, don't you think?"

Michelle didn't even know the meaning of the word. Harsh was when you discovered your sister had been lying to you. Harsh was when you realized the man you loved could never love you back. How could he, with so much in the way...

"Danni," said Michelle. "There isn't trouble in paradise, is there?"

Danni winced. "And what paradise would that be?"

"You know. That absolutely gorgeous man who comes to see you at the office now and then. I mean, obviously something's going on between the two of you." Michelle got a soulful look. "Maybe *I've* had my heart broken, but I want other people to be happy."

Larry made an unintelligible sound. Michelle drew her eyebrows together and went on.

"My experience with Mr. Nolan taught me a lot, Danni. It taught me not to take any moment of happiness for granted."

Danni wondered how on earth Michelle could have gained anything profound from the fact that ninety-nine percent of the time, Mr. Nolan had ignored her very existence. She could tell Larry was wondering the same thing.

''Michelle,'' Danni said, ''sentiment appreciated and all, but we do need to narrow down the field here a bit. We are knee-deep in these blasted horses.''

''You know,'' Michelle said thoughtfully. ''When you love the wrong person, everything else in your life is wrong. But if you find the *right* person...everything else has to be right, too, doesn't it?'' Her gaze lingered just for a second or two on Larry, then skittered away.

''Admirable logic,'' Danni muttered. But this time Michelle's words struck home.

Danni had found the right man to love. It was just too bad *she* was the wrong one for him.

CHAPTER THIRTEEN

BRYAN WAS CELEBRATING. Or, more accurately, C. J. Whitfield was celebrating and Bryan was just along for the ride. These days he didn't seem to feel much of anything—a certain numbness had taken him over.

"I'm very glad," said C.J., raising her wineglass, "that we finally came to an agreement. The agreement being that I am going to invest an outrageous amount of money in your project."

Cause for celebration, indeed. Bryan wished he could feel more excited about it. But the numbness seemed to blanket everything, like a thick protective fog. He supposed he was grateful for it. If he didn't feel the good things, he didn't feel the bad, either.

He still didn't know what had changed C.J.'s mind. But she'd called him up, announced that she wanted to do business with him and they'd spent the morning discussing the figures. The contract was all but signed—which was why they sat at a very popular downtown Italian restaurant.

"Bryan, you're still so far away," C.J. complained. "I thought my money at least would have an effect. I try to lure you to my bed—that doesn't work. What *is* it going to take?"

She seemed to bear remarkably little resentment about the other night, when he'd walked away from her. But right now that night seemed like a million years ago. So much had happened since.

He tried to gather some enthusiasm, and raised his glass to hers. She leaned against him, smiling into his eyes. He untwined her hand from his arm. Good-naturedly she twined it right back. Romantic music played in the background, but he wasn't in the mood. They were at a window seat, and he looked outside for some distraction. Lord. That was when he saw Danni and Kristine coming across the street, right toward the restaurant, their arms laden with packages. It still threw him when he observed them together like this. The identical blond hair, identical heart-shaped faces...two women—mirror images of each other. But he had a pretty good idea he could tell them apart by the way they were dressed: Kristine in one of those designer outfits she seemed to like, and Danni in khaki pants, hiking shirt and tennis shoes. His gaze lingered on Danni, and then he raised a hand in greeting.

Neither one of them waved back. Kristine scowled at him. Danni seemed to be studying the way C. J. Whitfield was snaking her arm across his shoulders. He unsnaked it, but she promptly put it back.

Kristine came striding into the restaurant, Danni a pace or two behind. Both of them stopped in front of his table.

''Hello, there,'' Bryan said.

C.J. swiveled her head from one twin to the other. ''Wow,'' she said under her breath.

Kristine gave both of them a regal glance, then centered her gaze on Bryan. ''Really,'' she said. ''Bryan, how could *you*...the father of both our children...be dating another woman!'' And with that, she swept out of the restaurant again, dragging Danni with her. Danni glanced back at him with something like horrified curiosity, but Kristine whipped her right out the door and both of them vanished.

For a minute C.J. didn't speak. She just sat there looking stunned. But then she snatched her arm away from him and scrambled to her feet.

"There's actually an explanation," Bryan said. "Sort of, anyway."

"I don't want to hear it, Bryan. I really don't." She backed away from him as if he possessed some lunacy that might be catching. "Don't call me, I'll call you. I think you get the idea."

"I think so," he said.

C.J.'s assistant materialized and escorted her boss away. C.J. didn't look back even once.

The waiter came over and gave him a look that was half sympathetic, half admiring. "Guess you won't be having dessert," he said.

"Apparently not." Bryan paid the check and made his own exit. For some reason he was reminded of a circus sideshow.

Except that right now he felt more like the main-ring event.

BRYAN HAD INTENDED to meet Kristine on neutral ground—someplace where he could tell her what was on his mind. She wasn't making it easy, however. She'd shown up at Balboa Park in what could only be called a jogging ensemble: bright-pink leotards, a fashionably oversize T-shirt that had probably never seen a drop of sweat in its life and a pink bandana. And she was wearing a lot of makeup...too much of the stuff. Obviously she'd gone to a lot of effort. And that was going to make it a lot harder to rake her over the coals.

''About the scene you pulled yesterday,'' he began gruffly.

''I know, Bryan, I know,'' she said in a repentant tone. ''I went much too far, didn't I? Swooping down on you in the restaurant that way. Afterward...I don't know what got into me!''

She was almost making him feel sorry for her. How the hell had she managed that?

''Kris,'' he tried again. ''You cost me an investor. A really important one.''

''I'm sorry,'' she said miserably. ''It's just that I took one look at you with that woman...and I didn't think *investor.* I thought...well, I guess I *wasn't* thinking, was I?''

An understatement. ''So,'' Bryan said. ''You ruin my professional life. Not to mention my personal life—''

''Have I ruined it, Bryan?'' she asked. ''Would it be so horrible if...if this baby did turn out to be yours...?''

He was getting a surreal feeling. The feeling

that said this couldn't be happening to him. Not just two sisters anymore. Two babies. Lord. His life was getting more crowded by the minute.

Seeing the irony in the situation didn't help. Nothing helped. He started jogging, expecting Kristine to keep pace beside him. Instead she dropped back.

"Slow down for a moment, will you, Bryan?" she panted.

At this rate, he felt like he was running in place. Maybe he shouldn't have asked Kristine to meet him here, after all. This park was a favorite retreat of his—acres of grass and trees, and the old Spanish buildings here and there. Now he felt as if he had no place left to retreat.

"Why the hell did you lie in the first place?" he asked.

"Which lie?" she murmured sorrowfully. "I've committed so many of them...."

She was trying to play on his sympathies again. She'd fouled up big time, and she wanted him to comfort *her.* The surreal feeling came over him once more.

"Let's see," he said. "The part where you pretended to be your sister. The part where you said you were on birth control...while still pretending to be Danni. The part where you never said you were married. Do I about have it all covered?''

''Pretty much. I know there aren't any excuses.'' She sounded subdued now. And, dammit, her tactics were succeeding. He did feel the slightest stirring of sympathy.

''Bryan, for what it's worth...if I could just explain,'' she continued hesitantly. ''When I walked in that day, and found my husband with another woman...it was just so awful. Like the earth had suddenly shifted beneath my feet, and nothing would ever be the same again. Have you ever felt that way?''

''You might say so,'' he remarked dryly.

''Oh, right. Because of...me.'' She glanced away guiltily. ''Anyway, I know I can't justify what I did. It's just that...ever since that day with Ted, I've felt...lost. The world still shifting every time I take a step. And I guess...I guess when I'm with you...that's the only time I don't feel that way.''

She was playing on his sympathies, all right—big time. He didn't like it. But he also didn't know what the hell to do about it.

HOBBYHORSE TOYS was really getting into the Christmas spirit. The company executives had decided that in addition to the rocking-horse competition, they would sponsor a free trip to Sea World for ten lucky children. Danni, of course, was obliged to come along in order to handle publicity. So far she'd posed the kids by the dolphins, the otters and the penguins, the photographer snapping away. At last, after a long while, she was able to take a welcome break next to the starfish. There was something very restful about starfish. You had to look at them for the longest time just to see if they moved. She wished she could be that motionless, that peaceful.

"Hello, Danni."

She whirled at the sound of Bryan's voice, her heart pounding absurdly. "What on earth—"

His eyes captured hers. "It took some doing to find you. First I called your office. Somebody named Melissa, I think—"

"Michelle," Danni said grimly. "*She* told you where I was."

"It still wasn't easy after that," he remarked. "This is a big place. But finally somebody told me where to find the Hobbyhorse contingent...and here I am."

"Obviously," Danni muttered. She couldn't help her gaze traveling over him. Today he was casual again, wearing jeans and a T-shirt. It was almost unlawful, how attractive he looked....

Danni forced herself to concentrate on matters at hand. "You've gone to a lot of trouble to find me, and I don't understand why."

"A little something about you refusing to answer my calls. I got the impression you were home last night...but you just kept letting the answering machine pick up."

Danni folded her arms tightly, digging her fingernails into her skin. Anything to keep from reaching out to touch him as she longed to do. "If that was the impression you got—it should have told you something, Bryan."

"Why don't you want to talk to me, Danni? Is it what you saw yesterday?"

Danni shivered, even though it wasn't cold. "I'm not even sure what I saw," she muttered. "There Kris and I were, minding our own business, doing our Christmas shopping. We look across the street, see *you* with some giddy brunette...who knows what it's all about."

"I don't think C. J. Whitfield has ever been called giddy before," he said thoughtfully.

"Oh, so that's her name. Well, I hope the two of you will be very happy. Just try not to get *her* in the family way." She wished that last bit hadn't popped out. It made her feel silly and spiteful.

"No chance of that," Bryan said. "C.J. and I aren't exactly close."

"You could have fooled me," Danni said, turning back to the starfish.

"If you'd looked more carefully," Bryan told her, "you would have seen C.J. making overtures...and me not."

She wanted desperately to believe him. But there was so much else wrong between them!

"In fact, we were about to close a business deal," Bryan explained. "Until your sister put in her two cents' worth, that is."

Danni wondered if she would ever stop feeling guilty over Kristine's excesses. Why did she have to keep blaming herself for them?

"I wish I'd stopped her, Bryan. But she surprised even me. Unfortunately, my reaction time isn't what it should be these days."

"I guess it's not easy," he said, "trying to be your sister's keeper."

She sighed. "No it's not. And meanwhile...I wish you hadn't come here, Bryan. I'm very busy."

He glanced across at the brood of kids. They all seemed to be darting in different directions, threatening to escape the beleaguered parents who had volunteered to come along with them.

"So that's what happens when one has kids," he said, as if to himself.

"They're excited. Of course they're a little unruly." She didn't know why she was defending kids who weren't her own. "Bryan, I'm sure you've seen children before."

"It's different now...it's just different."

"Anyway," she continued, "you've found me, you've explained about your luncheon date, and—"

"It wasn't a date," he said, sounding disgruntled. "Like I told you—it was a business meeting."

"Right—a business meeting that we ruined for you." Danni concentrated on those starfish. Such a lovely orangy color, and so blessedly inert...

Suddenly one of the little boys in the group began sprinting off. Danni hurried after him and grabbed his hand. "They're just the opposite of starfish," she muttered. "They move *too* fast."

The little boy studied Bryan. "Who are you?" he asked. Bryan introduced himself gravely. And then, quite easily and naturally, he introduced himself to the little boy's father. Everybody seemed to hit it off. What could Danni do after that? Bryan, scarcely trying, had become part of their little group. Some of the kids started to hang on to him.

"He's mine," said a six-year-old girl named Samantha, grabbing his free hand.

"He's *mine,*" said a five-year-old named Lauren, latching on to his arm.

Danni almost laughed. Would females always be in competition over Bryan McKay? But she had to admit he was good with children. He stopped at the exhibits with them, listening seriously to the convoluted stories the kids told him, showing no apparent sign of impatience. And that only sent another stab of longing and pain through Danni. How on earth were they ever going to resolve their impossible situation?

Bryan even agreed to be in some of the photographs. Danni imagined a picture of him in the newspaper, surrounded by a flock of kids. "Just wait," she told him, "until C. J. Whitfield gets a load of *that.*"

Bryan gave her a sardonic look, but refrained from comment.

By the end of the day, the children were invariably tired and cranky, but a couple of them were still reluctant to let go of Bryan. He turned them over to their parents with aplomb, and then approached Danni.

"Can we get out of here now?" he asked.

She glanced at her watch. "You can certainly get out. But I'm going back to the office—"

"No, you're not." He took her hand and began leading her away. "We're going to eat dinner."

"I'm not hungry just yet," she protested.

"Don't you need protein, or whatever?" His gaze strayed to her stomach.

"Oh, for goodness' sake." Danni tugged away from him indignantly. "I can handle things myself."

"You keep saying that. But you look worn out *and* hungry."

She couldn't deny that what he said was true. She felt like one of the kids—tired and cranky and just wanting to go home. It amazed her that on the outside her pregnancy seemed to show no sign as yet, even as it sapped every bit of her energy on the inside.

"So let's eat," Bryan said.

"Because I'm a mother-to-be, and I need fattening up?" Danni said sarcastically.

"No. Because you're...Danni."

Somehow that was reason enough to give in.

THEY ATE AT a restaurant on the bay. The sky had turned lavender with the approaching night, and the waters had darkened. Sailboats shifted against their moorings. Danni remembered the day Bryan had taken her to Coronado Island in his own boat. Even then the heartache had already begun. Would it ever leave her?

She took a bite of sea bass. Under other circumstances, she probably would have found the meal delicious: endive salad with honey-mustard dressing, wild rice and roasted peppers, flaky rolls with whipped butter.

Bryan didn't seem to be having any problem with *his* appetite.

"Have a good time today?" she asked.

"Yeah...I think I did." He sounded surprised.

"It almost seemed like a normal afternoon, didn't it?" she continued.

"Normal," he said. "I don't know what the hell is normal anymore."

"Bryan," she said, taking a deep breath, "I think you do. You want to know what really bothered me about seeing you with C. J. Whitfield yesterday?"

"Let's forget C.J.," he said.

"What really bothered me," Danni persisted,

"was realizing you *could* have a normal relationship with some other woman."

"As opposed to an abnormal one with you?" Bryan asked, leaning back in his chair.

"I'm not making a joke," Danni said severely. "I'm trying to tell you something important. Namely, you ought to go find yourself somebody...*normal.* If it's not this C.J. person, then it will be somebody else. You'll know her when you see her."

"I get it," Bryan said. "She won't have a twin running amuck somewhere. And that will make her...normal."

"I wouldn't actually accuse Kris of running amuck," Danni began. Then she listened to herself and stopped. "Anyway, you get my meaning."

Now Bryan reached across the table and clasped her hand. It was the lightest touch, but it sent a tingling response all through her.

"Danni," he murmured, "I don't want somebody normal. Right now all I want is you."

His eyes told her that he was only kidding about the "normal" part. They also told her what he was thinking about next. She was thinking about it, too. Making love...

"Bryan, we can't—"

“Why not?” he asked reasonably. And then the hint of a smile. “The damage has already been done. We might as well enjoy ourselves.”

Her face grew hot. “Our lives are more of a mess than ever, and you want to jump into…”

“Bed,” he finished for her.

Oh, how she wanted it, too. How she wanted *him.* His closeness, his caresses. But afterward her heart would break into even smaller pieces.

Impossible. It’s always like this—everything between us so impossible.

She withdrew her hand from his. “I’m sorry, Bryan,” she said quietly. “But we both know sex isn’t going to solve anything.”

“I wasn’t looking for a solution. I just want to be with you, Danni.”

“No,” she said, scarcely above a whisper now. “I can’t do this anymore. It’s too painful.”

“What, Danni?” He gazed at her intently.

“Being with you in any way. Knowing that everything’s only going to get worse—not better. I’d rather make a break. A clean one.” Her voice gathered a welcome strength.

“What exactly are you saying, Danni?”

She set down her napkin and stood. “I’m saying that it’s over, Bryan. Once and for all—it’s over. You know what? It's the only way. There *is* no other solution."

He frowned. "I disagree."

"You don't have any choice." How calm she suddenly felt, calm and sure. "I'm telling you goodbye, Bryan. And I'm telling you…I never want to see you again."

CHAPTER FOURTEEN

HUNTING FOR investors was hard work, especially when your heart wasn't in it. It was also the Christmas season. Not exactly a good time to be asking people for money.

By eleven o'clock in the morning, Bryan gave up and headed for the gym. It was a boxing gym, in one of San Diego's more questionable neighborhoods. Bryan didn't get down here as often as he'd like, but today he definitely needed to let off some steam.

He already had his gloves on and he was headed for the ring when he saw her. *Danni.* She stood in the doorway, glancing around.

She'd changed her mind. Yesterday hadn't been good-bye, after all.

He went toward her. And then it hit. She was wearing one of those silk dresses and shoes with the heels too high. Danni would never wear a getup like that.

The disappointment thumped him like a physical blow. He masked his expression, but apparently too late. He could tell she saw. Her cheeks burned with color.

"You thought I was Danni."

"Hello, Kris. How'd you find me?"

"Your assistant. She took a little chatting up, but she finally relented and told me where you were."

He'd have to have a talk with Jeanine.

"What can I do for you?" he asked Kristine.

"So formal," she chided, the flirtatious manner back in place. "I just decided I needed to see more of your life, Bryan." She glanced around, taking in the scarred walls, the low ceiling, the barred windows. "It's oppressive in here. How about escaping with me?"

He thought how differently Danni would have reacted. She would have been curious, asking questions about the gym and the neighborhood. She'd probably understand why he liked the place. Bryan had started coming here when he was a sophomore in high school. At first the idea had been to learn how to defend himself against some older guys intent on beating the hell out of him. But then it had become something more. Here the things that counted were skill and strength and physical endurance. Once he'd proven he had those, he'd been accepted.

"Bryan...*could* we get out of here?" Kristine said distastefully. The atmosphere of the place had changed subtly since her entrance. The other guys were staring at her appreciatively. There was no hope for Bryan getting a decent workout, after all.

"Sure," he said. "Come on—let's go."

She sent a quizzical glance at his shorts and ragged T-shirt. "Don't you have to change?"

"I'll be coming back."

"What am I allotted?" she asked. "Five minutes—ten?"

He realized he'd hurt her feelings. You never knew how your words would affect Kristine. Danni was different...with Danni, conversation was easy. You didn't have to think about every damn thing you said.

He and Kristine went out to the street. Once again she glanced at his attire.

"I'm confused about something," she said lightly. "Danni always tells me that you accept nothing but the best. So why the ratty T-shirt? It looks like it should be condemned."

"It is the best," he told her. "It's my favorite." He'd had it for a very long time and he kept extending its life span, ignoring the new holes that formed.

"I get the feeling you didn't just come down here to critique my fashion sense," he told her. "What's up?"

"Obviously I'm supposed to get right to the point." She glanced around at the shabby store-fronts. "I *will* tell you—but couldn't we go someplace a little more inviting?"

He didn't answer.

"Okay, okay, I get the message. I've already disrupted your life enough by coming here. And by everything else I've done... I deserve having you angry at me, I know that."

The numbness was back, the sense that nothing mattered much one way or the other. So why not take her where she wanted?

"I'm parked over there." He nodded toward his car.

She climbed into the passenger seat. He got behind the wheel and turned the key.

"No—wait," she said. "Let's just sit here. It's kind of nice, isn't it?" She sounded anxious, as if asking for his approval on some deeper level.

"Sure, Kris."

She leaned back against the headrest. "I

thought we should talk about us, Bryan. I mean...we do have to talk about it, don't we?''

Bryan grimaced a little. He wanted to tell her that there was no ''us.'' He couldn't though, because of one small detail. He could be the father of her baby.

''Are you okay, Bryan?''

He rubbed his neck. ''I'm fine,'' he said. ''Just a reminder, Kris... If I'd known you had a husband...not to mention if I'd known you weren't Danni—''

''Right. Understood.'' She rushed on. ''The thing is, Bryan, my marriage really is over. I don't have any hope left for it at all. And that means...it means I have to start divorce proceedings pretty soon. That's a step in the right direction, isn't it?'' Her voice was heavy—but she also sounded as if she were seeking his guidance on the matter.

''Look, Kris,'' he said, ''I'm sorry.'' He actually meant it.

She turned toward him. The car seemed too small, Kristine too close. But she gazed at him intently, as if she had something important to say.

''Bryan...I guess there's no other way to do this, except to say it straight out. You must know how I feel about you. And...as soon as my divorce is final...I want to marry you!"

Her words hung there in the air, impossible to avoid. She gazed at him so hopefully. So trustfully, almost, as if she thought he would solve everything that had happened...everything she'd done. She was working on his sympathies again, but this time he couldn't let it get to him. For the first time in a long while, he knew exactly what he needed to say.

"Kris, it's not going to happen. I think you know that already. As far as the baby...I'll be a part of his life...or her life...any way I can. I'll be a father, the best one I can be. But I can't be your husband."

She stared at him, a wounded look on her face. And, in spite of everything she'd done, in spite of everything she'd caused, she got to him. He felt the sympathy.

But it didn't change anything.

IT WAS TWO DAYS before Christmas, and the grand winner of the rocking-horse competition was about to be announced. Danni, Michelle and Larry had at last decided on a most impressive specimen: a horse carved of beechwood, mane and tail so intricately fashioned they seemed to be flying in the wind. And it wore a bright first-prize ribbon around its neck.

Danni sat on a podium at the Hobbyhorse Toys factory. Larry was on one side of her, Michelle the other. That photographer was snapping away again—more publicity photos. Michelle kept sneaking glances toward Larry. Larry kept sneaking glances back. It was getting to be very aggravating.

''Anything I should know about?'' Danni asked.

Michelle pretended to flip through the file in her lap. ''Nothing,'' she said.

Larry pretended to yawn, and didn't say anything at all. Something was up, all right. Maybe the two of them had gone on a date. Who knew. Maybe they'd declared eternal love to each other—anything was possible. At least Danni didn't have to listen to Michelle maunder on about Mr. Nolan anymore.

The almighty Mr. Nolan, in fact, had shown up personally for today's ceremony. He, too, sat on the podium, but Michelle seemed oblivious to him. Miracles did happen.

The festivities got under way. A speech or two by Hobbyhorse executives. Mr. Nolan taking a bow. And Danni standing to award first place to a seventy-five-year-old man who'd been wood-carving in his spare time for over six decades. The appropriate applause from the audience, lightbulbs flashing yet again. And then, mercifully, it was over. At last she could think about going home.

Mr. Nolan intercepted her. "Good job, Doreen," he said magnanimously.

She stared, wondering if she'd heard right. "Doreen?"

"Excellent work," he said, and walked away. All this time, Danni had told herself that the man was so oblivious, he didn't even know Michelle's name. The joke was on her—apparently he didn't know *her* name, either.

Danni stared after him. It all seemed so clear right now. She was doing a job she hated...working for somebody who didn't even know her. All in all, she was an executive on her way to a major ulcer.

Something had to give.

DANNI HAD NEVER cared for her sister's house in Sugar Beach. It stood at the crest of a wide expanse of lawn, columns rising like some misplaced Southern mansion. It was too pretentious, too ornate. Danni rang the doorbell, wishing she didn't have to be here.

Ted himself answered. "Thank you for coming, Danni," he said formally, ushering her inside.

Ted had always had a quiet, reflective manner, a pleasing contrast to Kristine's exuberance. But there was no Kristine at the house anymore, and it seemed too cavernous without her.

In the living room, Danni saw that Ted had put up the Christmas tree—white-frosted limbs reaching to the ceiling. He followed the direction of Danni's glance.

"I never did like that tree much," he said glumly. "I guess I always pictured going out to the woods and finding some tree with scraggly branches that needed a good home. And after Christmas, planting it in the front yard. But Kris asked me to imagine a yard filled with Christmas trees from years past. She said it would look absurd. I always thought it would look...nice."

Danni really didn't want to hear about Ted and Kristine's disagreements. She'd only come here today because Ted had made it sound so urgent.

"So, Ted," she said briskly. "What can I do for you?"

He didn't answer. Instead he began rooting around in a box of Christmas ornaments. He held one up. "Remember this, Danni?"

She examined the little rag snowman, with his striped muffler and his stovepipe hat made of black felt.

"Yes, I remember," she said. "That was the year you and Kris were first together. You actually went to the flea market to look for Christmas ornaments. Kris made you go. She couldn't believe you'd never been to a flea market before. You found the snowman…and this." Danni rooted around in the box herself, coming up with a rosy-cheeked papier-mâché Santa. His red hat had torn just a bit, but he still looked jaunty.

"I wonder what happened to us," Ted murmured, gazing at the ornaments. "I keep asking myself that question, over and over."

Danni made an effort, and restrained from offering some remark about Ted's affair getting in the way. Instead she opened a box of silver bulbs, and started hanging them on the tree. After a moment, Ted started unwinding the wooden cranberry strings.

An hour later, they'd made considerable progress. "Thanks, Danni," he said.

"Somehow I don't think you asked me over

for a tree-decorating party,'' she told him. ''I'm ready to listen, if you have something to say.''

''I want you to tell Kris to stop acting like a self-indulgent drama queen.''

The description was hardly flattering, but accurate. Danni sat down in Kristine's favorite armchair, the one with needlepoint upholstery. ''I don't think it's a good idea for me to get involved in this,'' she said carefully. ''Besides, I've already tried talking to her. I've tried to convince her she should at least give the two of you a chance to work things out.''

''And what happened?''

Danni tried to put it in diplomatic terms. ''She pretty much...blew up.''

Ted nodded. ''That sounds like Kris. She refuses even to listen—even to consider my side of the story.''

Danni reminded herself not to get involved. But then she couldn't help herself. ''Well, Ted, there is the little matter of you still being involved with your neighbor. Someone by the name of Alex Peterson, I believe Kris said.''

Ted looked genuinely puzzled. ''Still involved...where did she get that idea?''

''From Alex herself, it seems. The lady came to see Kris, and said she loved you, and you loved her…or some such. And naturally Kris didn't feel reassured."

He shook his head, uttering an expressive curse. "The woman was flat-out lying. I broke it off the same day Kris walked in and—anyway, I broke it off right then. But if Kris thinks otherwise…no wonder she's been slamming the phone in my ear."

Danni stood. It seemed Kristine wasn't the only one with a flair for fiction. Alex Peterson might just be her match. "Sounds like you have something to talk to Kris about. Guess my job here is done. I'll see myself out—"

"Wait, Danni. You can't go yet. I still need you to…mediate."

She didn't like the sound of that. "Really, Ted. Work it out between the two of you."

"She won't listen to me," he said in a clipped tone. "I'm asking you to talk to her again. You're her sister, the person she trusts more than any other. Eventually she'll have to pay attention."

Danni raised her hands in a gesture of frustration. "Ted, don't get me wrong. I'm very glad you still want to get back together with Kris. But it's no use coming to me. *You're* the one who has to convince her."

"How?" The single word was stark.

Danni searched for an answer. "You just start from the beginning, I suppose. You keep telling her how sorry you are, until at last she believes you. And then of course she says she's sorry, too, for trying to get even through Bryan. And as for the baby—"

"What?" Now Ted's voice sounded oddly hoarse. "What baby? And who's Bryan? What are you talking about?"

Danni felt an ominous sinking sensation. "Kris said she'd told you everything. And I just thought…I thought you were being understanding about it all, because you were the one who had an affair first…." She wanted frantically to stop the words from tumbling out of her mouth, and at last she managed it. But it was too late. Ted's face had already turned white. It was very clear he hadn't known a thing about Bryan. Or the baby.

Moving almost unsteadily, he went to a chair and sat down. "Do you mind running that by me again?" he said in a strangely polite voice.

Danni couldn't tell him no, not after what she'd just done to him. Not for the first time, she cursed her sister. She tried to be as succinct and clear as possible, but that didn't make the whole thing any less dreadful.

If possible, Ted looked even more shocked than Bryan had when he'd heard the news.

"Let me get this straight," he muttered. "You and Kristine are both pregnant. And the father is...the same guy."

"Not necessarily," Danni said. "I think we're all pretty much hoping that you're the father of Kris's baby."

"Good Lord," Ted uttered under his breath.

"She said you knew," Danni murmured. "I didn't know she was lying about that, too...."

"Maybe she's lying about...about going to bed with the guy—"

"Sorry," Danni said. "That much at least is true. She was pretending to be me, and—you know, Ted, I just don't think I can talk about this anymore. You know what I mean?"

"Yeah," he said. "I know what you mean."

DANNI SAT at the kitchen table in her parents' house. Some families used the kitchen as an informal gathering place, where all sorts of cozy clutter accumulated—magnets and children's' pictures sprouting on the refrigerator door, cookie cutters and mixing bowls crowding the counters, potted plants taking over the windowsill. The Ferris kitchen, however, was something else entirely. There was clutter, all right, but it was always the serious variety: law books and business journals spread out on the table, notes from work tacked to the bulletin board, a cell phone or two residing in the china cabinet next to the second-best plates. Jay and Leah Ferris lived and breathed their careers. They expected Danni to do the same.

At this very moment, in fact, Danni's father was working late, and Leah Ferris had just arrived home from her own office. Danni felt very nervous, sitting here across from her mother, knowing that she was about to go from family success story to family problem. Being an unwed mother would do that to you. But the cat was out of the bag, so to speak—she'd had to tell Ted about her pregnancy, and that meant she couldn't keep it from her parents.

Leah took a sip of coffee. "Are you sure you don't want any?" she asked.

"I'm staying away from caffeine these days."

Leah gave her a sharp glance. "Really. That's not like you—haven't you always joked that it takes a gallon of coffee to fill up your tank?"

Another badge of the harried professional. But

maybe it was time to announce her news. Danni's apprehension crescendoed.

"Mom...I'm pregnant."

Leah didn't say a word at first. If she was shocked or disappointed, she didn't let on.

"I'm just trying to assimilate it all," she said at last. "A baby...wow."

"That was my reaction," Danni admitted. "Wow...a baby."

"I must admit," Leah said, "it's something of a surprise. Make that a major surprise. But I suppose there's only one thing that really matters. Are you happy, Danni?"

Somehow it was the question Danni would least have expected. She was grateful for it.

"About the baby...yes, I'm happy. Ninety percent of the time, anyway. The other ten percent I'm petrified."

"Welcome to motherhood," Leah said in a rueful tone. "The proportions will change now and then, of course...."

Her mother acted as if she were welcoming her into some difficult but prestigious club. It all seemed too good to be true.

"You're taking this very well," Danni said.

"Oh, Danni...do you think I've never dreamed of having a grandchild someday? Of course I have. And if you're fine with it...believe me, I'll spoil the kid rotten. Meanwhile, I don't suppose you'd want to share any information about the father.''

Danni felt herself clench inside. The very mention of Bryan sent longing and sadness through her.

''He's a good person,'' Danni said at last. ''It's just that...for unavoidable reasons...he can't be part of my life. It's not his choosing. It's...mine.'' No way was she going to spring the news about *Kristine* on her mother. She'd already told *that* story once today. Kristine would have to let the rest of the family in on it—and that would happen soon enough. Right now Danni was giving Leah more than enough to handle.

But Leah took in the latest with aplomb also. ''I trust your opinion where men are concerned. That dreadful Peter excepted, you've always shown intelligent judgment. And thank goodness you have such a secure job. You'll need it, especially at a time like this.''

Danni had to get it all over at once. ''Actually, Mom...I'm thinking about quitting my job.''

''Please tell me you're joking,'' Leah said.

"No joke. I'm serious."

"I just don't believe it," Leah said. "Whatever's wrong with you, Danni? All the work you've put in to get where you are! The successes you've achieved."

This, in the end, was typical Leah. She'd taken it right in stride to learn that her daughter was pregnant, with no plans to have the father of the baby around. But one mention of the fact that Danni might walk out of Nolan, Williams and Beck, and all calm had disintegrated.

Leah couldn't even seem to sit still anymore. She stood and began pacing between the counter and the table.

"You'll have to explain this to me, because I just don't understand. It doesn't make any sense. Of course, *I'm* the first one to admit that the hormones of pregnancy can unbalance a person a little. So what you do is—you put the thought right out of your head."

"Mom, hold on," Danni said. "I'll explain, if you'd just listen—"

"Your father and I have always been so proud of you, Danni."

"That's just the thing," Danni rushed on, before her mother could get another word in. "All my life I've tried so hard to please you—especially when it comes to my career. But I *hate* advertising. I despise it. Sometimes I don't think I can take another minute of it."

At last she seemed to be getting through to her mother. Leah sat down once more.

"Are you saying that we coerced you, Danni? Because all we ever wanted was for you to have some security and some...some success. And we never specifically said go into advertising. That was your idea, all along—"

"I know, Mom," Danni said earnestly. "I'm not blaming you. I'm just saying that now it's time for a change. Having this baby has made me realize that. It's just...shaken me up about everything. It's made me realize I have to choose something that makes me happy."

Leah picked up her coffee cup and took a gulp as if *she* needed a major dose of caffeine.

"Danni, you have so much to think about. How will you support a baby if you quit? Have you even considered that?"

"Yes, Mom," Danni said as patiently as possible. "I have a couple of ideas I'm tossing around—"

"But nothing, I'm sure, as secure as the job you have now. The *career* you have now, Danni." Leah gave her a meaningful look. And

Danni knew it was useless to talk any more. The supreme irony remained. Her mother would accept her as an unwed mother. But mess with her career…no way.

CHAPTER FIFTEEN

"DANNI, HOW COULD YOU? What were you thinking? Why did you spill the beans to Ted!" No sooner had Kristine burst into Danni's office, than she assaulted her with these staccato demands. Danni calmly went on organizing the contents of her desk.

"Gee," she said. "I guess I thought *you'd* told Ted you'd had an affair. But where would I get an idea like that?"

Kristine plunked herself down on the edge of the desk, sending papers flying. "You can forget the sarcasm. That day I was upset. I was just saying anything that popped into my head! I hadn't really told him. But now he's saying *he'll* never forgive *me*."

"Guess you'd call that a taste of your own medicine," Danni said. She tossed a bottle of antacid tablets into the trash can. If she did leave Nolan, Williams and Beck, she wouldn't be needing those anymore. Might as well start getting used to the idea now.

"Danni, please pay attention. My life is in ruins, and you didn't help."

Danni studied her sister. "I wonder when the lying is going to stop," she said. "You're behaving exactly like that woman, Alex Peterson. She lied about still being involved with Ted. And you've lied about pretty much everything, Kris. So, the question remains. When is it going to stop?"

Kristine got a defeated look. "Do you think I admire myself? I get to feeling so desperate…and things happen."

"They don't just happen. You make them happen." Danni started making a stack of paper clips that had gotten stuck in odd corners of her desk. At last Kristine stirred out of her self-involved reverie.

"Danni…what are you doing?" she asked apprehensively.

"Cleaning up. Cleaning out. Because I'm thinking about leaving this place far, far behind." Danni unearthed a calendar at the bottom of one of the drawers. It was two years out of date. If she continued to work here, more years of her life would get lost at the bottom of some drawer.

"You can't be serious," Kristine exclaimed. "To leave at a time like this—when you're going to have a family to support!"

"You and me both," Danni said, gathering up loose rubber bands. Then she glanced speculatively at her sister. "Of course, how do I even know you *are* pregnant, Kris?"

Kris straightened, a look of outrage crossing her face now. "How could you even question that?"

"There have been so many other lies," Danni reminded her. "Why not that, too?"

She clenched her hands. "And why would I do something so horrible?"

"Plenty of reasons," Danni said. "To hurt your husband. To get Bryan."

Suddenly Kris seemed to deflate. She sank back onto the desk. "You make me sound so conniving. But it's not like that, Danni. The very first time I saw Bryan...and your name popped out of my mouth...I didn't plan it. I didn't come up with some master plot to ruin everybody's lives! And everything afterward... Saying things without thinking. Regretting them afterward. Getting myself in deeper and deeper."

That unwelcome sympathy for her sister began to stir. Danni tried as hard as she could to resist it. ‘‘I’m sorry, Kris, but I can’t be around you right now. I never really do know when you’re telling me the truth or not. So…maybe it would be better if we didn’t see each other for a little while.’’

Kristine shook her head in disbelief. ‘‘You’re cutting me off—your own sister?’’

‘‘Don’t make it sound so melodramatic,’’ Danni said. ‘‘I’m just asking for a little distance. And it will only be for a short while.’’ A pattern was emerging from the past twenty-four hours, and Danni finally understood it. She was like someone cleaning house—sweeping all the floors, opening all the windows. Clearing out her life, preparing as best she could for this baby’s arrival. She had to make her existence simple and strong. That meant time away from her sister. It probably meant quitting her job and finding more satisfying work. And, perhaps most of all, it meant no more contact with Bryan.

Her heart seemed to twist inside her at the thought. And another thought came to her, seeming to accuse.

A baby needs a father.

That was for ordinary situations. Danni’s,

however, was no ordinary case. She couldn't afford to weaken now, not with anyone.

"I think you need to leave, Kris."

Her sister looked mournful. "I've never seen you like this before. And I've always been able to count on you...."

"I'm not disowning you," Danni said patiently. "It's only for a little while. Until we're both stronger."

"There's only one problem," Kristine said. "I've never been strong without you." She began walking from the office, then paused and turned. "For whatever it's worth, Danni...I *am* pregnant." With that, she left.

Danni had never been more certain that she'd done the right thing. But she'd also never been more lonely.

DANNI HAD JUST CLIMBED into her hatchback when she glanced into her rearview mirror, and saw the little blue sports car pulling up behind her.

"Oh, no," she murmured. She hadn't seen Bryan since their encounter at Sea World...the day she'd told him that she never wanted to see him again.

She didn't think she could face him right now.

She was tempted to gun the engine and speed away. But already he was coming over to her side of the car, leaning down to gaze at her through the window.

"Hello, Danni."

She tightened her hands on the wheel. "Hello, Bryan. Sorry I can't stay to talk. I'm already late for an appointment."

"Business appointment?" he asked.

"Personal."

"No chance you could break it," he said.

She stared straight ahead out the windshield. "If you must know, it's a doctor's appointment."

He nodded gravely. Then he came around to the other side of the car, opened the door, and climbed into the passenger seat. Now Danni tapped her fingers impatiently on the wheel.

"What's the idea?" she asked.

"This is a...baby thing, right?" He said the word *baby* as if it were an explosive in danger of detonating if he didn't handle it just right.

"Yes," Danni said. "It's a *baby* thing. Nothing to concern yourself about, though. Very routine."

Bryan stayed right where he was. "Isn't the...father supposed to be involved?" He approached the word *father* even more cautiously than *baby*.

"I suppose under normal circumstances," Danni said, "some fathers do go to the doctor and all. But our circumstances are definitely not normal."

"No," Bryan said. "They're not." He still didn't budge.

"What are you going to do after this?" Danni asked caustically. "Go with Kris to *her* doctor?"

For a minute or two, Bryan seemed as if he might really get mad at her. But then he recovered.

"I've told Kris what she can expect from me," he said, his voice gruff. She recognized that tone—it meant he was expressing thoughts he'd rather keep to himself. "If the kid's mine, I'll be a father. And I'll do it right. But I turned down her proposal of marriage."

Danni stared at him. "Kris...*proposed* to you?"

"Yes."

"Something else she didn't bother to tell me," Danni muttered. "When is all this going to end?" Then the rest of Bryan's comment sank in. He'd turned Kristine down. Danni felt guilty at the dart of happiness and relief she felt.

"I'll admit something," Danni said. "I'm glad you and Kris don't seem on your way to...a romantic relationship."

"How could you ever think we were?" Bryan asked.

"I haven't known what to think," Danni said. "About anything."

"That makes two of us. Just start the damn car, Danni. I'm doing the best I can here."

That much was true. And so, at last, she pulled out into traffic.

TWENTY MINUTES LATER, Danni and Bryan sat in the doctor's waiting room. Danni wished she could have chosen any other time for an appointment—today the place was overflowing with pregnant women. She sneaked a glance at Bryan, and saw that he was looking a bit white.

There was one other man in the place. He sat across from Danni and Bryan, holding the hand of a woman with a belly so enormous she looked as if she could go into labor at any moment. Now Danni began to feel a bit overwhelmed. That was going to happen to *her.* She had the impulse to jump up and go sprinting out of the room, as if that would somehow delay the inevitable.

"You okay?" Bryan murmured.

"Just fine." She tried to bury her nose in a magazine, but the couple across from them made that impossible. The man kept grinning at Bryan in a conspiratorial fashion.

"When are you two due?" the woman asked Danni in a friendly but intrusive manner.

"Um...August sometime," Danni said. That sounded reassuringly far away, but the woman wouldn't let up.

"You're going natural, aren't you?"

"Natural?" Danni mumbled.

"As in natural childbirth, of course." Now the woman sounded a bit reproving.

"Actually haven't planned that far ahead." Danni lifted her magazine again.

"*We're* going natural," the woman said. "We are going to experience every emotion, every physical sensation. Nothing is going to escape us."

Danni was infinitely grateful when the nurse showed her into one of the examination rooms. Bryan came along with her, his expression stoic. She didn't know how much more of this she could take.

"Bryan," she said. "Can't you just wait outside for me in the car?"

"What, and miss all the fun?" he muttered. He sounded like someone facing an endurance test.

"You know," Danni said. "I'm scared witless, too."

"But you're going through with it," he said.

"Yeah...no matter *how* scared I get." At least now she could speak with utter conviction. She paused. "Did you hope I wouldn't go through with it?"

He pushed a hand through his hair. "Hell, Danni. I'm still just trying to get used to the idea. I thought maybe coming here would make it seem...real."

"Maybe a little too real," she told him. And he didn't argue with her.

The nurse came in. While she took Danni's blood pressure, her gaze kept straying admiringly toward Bryan. Well, no wonder. The man *was* gorgeous. No doubt he would pass along some of those gorgeous genes to his and Danni's child.

She wished she wouldn't keep thinking about that. It didn't make things any easier.

The nurse left, and Dr. Metzger came in. She

was a woman in her fifties, a mother of three herself, she told Danni, and a recent grandmother. She shook hands matter-of-factly with both Danni and Bryan. Then she chatted easily for a few minutes about her own brood, giving the impression that having children was the most common and ordinary thing in the world. It helped, just a little, to keep some of the terror away. No doubt Dr. Metzger had perfected her technique with many nervous mothers-to-be...and fathers-to-be.

"Now, Danni," the doctor said. "I'm glad you've come back to see me so soon. I understand you have some questions you wanted to ask me."

One of the reasons Danni had chosen Dr. Metzger was her willingness to entertain any and all queries. She gave you the sense that she had all the time in the world for you—regardless of all those other pregnant ladies in her waiting room. But having Bryan here made Danni feel exceptionally awkward. He continued to wear the expression of a man about to jump off a cliff without a parachute.

Danni took out her note card with the questions jotted down, and determinedly plowed through them. She'd been amazed at all the concerns that popped up once she knew she was pregnant. Little worries that might seem foolish to someone else suddenly loomed in her mind. Fears that if she didn't do things exactly right, somehow she'd hurt the baby...

Should she eat more red meat? Could she have ice cream? Should she continue to exercise? How fat would she get? Could she still have sex...? Danni's face got hot with that one, and she made a concerted effort not to look at Bryan.

Dr. Metzger dispensed with all of Danni's worries matter-of-factly. "But you'll have lots more of them," she said cheerfully. "Don't stew about them—just call or come talk to me." Then she sailed out again.

Bryan was starting to look slightly relieved. "I thought they'd make you put on one of those paper gowns, and you know..."

"That was last time," Danni said. "Believe me, Bryan, there is only so much I will let you participate in. Especially when the last thing you want to do is participate. So *why* did you insist on coming with me today?" Her own emotions were dangerously close to the surface. She stood up and got out of the doctor's office as quickly as possible. Thank goodness that annoying couple was no longer in the waiting room.

Bryan caught up to her at the car. "Give me a break, Danni. This is all still pretty new to me."

She leaned against the car. "Believe me, I realize that," she said. "It's new for me, too. I feel like...like a heifer on display at the county fair!"

"Don't forget," he said, "I've paid for my admission. I'm as involved with this as you are."

Danni took a deep breath, wishing it would steady her. "Look, Bryan, I'm sorry. That afternoon we were together...I didn't even think about..."

"I was there, Danni," he said, his voice low and brusque. "I was part of it, if you remember. Stop taking the whole damn thing on your own shoulders."

"Yes, but you had reason to think everything...everything was taken care of...." She gave a sigh of despair. "Oh, how did I let all of this happen?"

He came to her and took her in his arms. "I let it happen, too. I don't know what the hell is coming next...but I'm here."

She leaned against him, feeling his warmth and strength. If only it could be like this always—Bryan's arms around her, sustaining her...

It wouldn't be enough, though. Danni would want more from him. She'd want to hear him say that he loved her and no one else. She'd want his passion and his devotion. Quite simply, she'd want him to feel exactly the way *she* felt.

Slowly she extricated herself, and stood alone. "Look," she said, "your coming with me to the doctor today was a nice gesture. So...thanks."

"You think that's all it was?" he asked. "A gesture?"

"I'm not asking for anything else from you," she said. "I'm handling this perfectly well on my own—"

"You were really scared in there."

"Okay, I was," she burst out. "I've already admitted as much! But it's not going to stop me. I'm going to have the baby...*my* baby. I'm going to handle everything just fine. You saw what a great doctor I have—she'll get me through."

Bryan frowned. "You're supposed to have a coach, or something."

"Kris will do it." Danni gave a laugh that was treacherously close to hysteria. "Can you just see the two of us? We'll probably both be in labor at the same time, telling each other how to breathe.''

''It is an image that boggles the imagination,'' Bryan said. He definitely had that traumatized look again, but he went on manfully. ''The point is, I'm worried about you, Danni.''

''Well, don't be. I am handling all of this just fine.'' She knew the more she repeated that, the less convincing she'd be. With an effort, she made herself shut up. She got into the car, snapped on her seat belt and started the engine. Bryan leaned down to peer through the window again.

''Aren't you forgetting something?'' he asked.

''No. What?'' Her fingers inched toward the gearshift knob.

''You gave me a ride here.''

''Oh, for goodness' sake.'' Danni flushed in embarrassment. ''Well, climb in then.''

Nothing was going right today. She wondered bleakly if anything ever would again.

BRYAN WAS LIKE a ghost haunting the house. He couldn't seem to find rest or peace anywhere. Always the memories assailed him. His mother, scouring and scrubbing until her fingers chapped. His own boyhood self, filled with resentment. And Danni, too…making love to her in this place. That, if anything, should have erased the bad memories. But it hadn't.

A knock came at the front door. He looked at the clock and saw that she was right on time. He went to open the door, and saw Danni standing on the porch.

"I'm glad you agreed to come," he said. After their visit to the doctor's office this morning, he thought maybe she'd written him off again. Maybe he hadn't handled it very well.

Now Danni stepped past Bryan, carrying her blueprints, and he caught her perfume…fresh, womanly. Sexy. But he didn't think she'd take too kindly to any overtures right now.

"I wondered if you were even going to show," he said.

"This will be quick," she answered in a no-nonsense tone. "I understand that you want to come to some resolution about the house. If I can help…why not?" She sounded very distant, very businesslike. Kneeling on the floor, she rolled out the blueprints.

"I've made modifications," she said, "based

on what we've discussed. You can show these to any contractor, and they'll know what to do."

"You should be finishing the job yourself," he said.

She gave him a skeptical glance. "You know that wouldn't work, Bryan. It would just be too awkward."

"A little late to be worried about awkward," he told her.

She looked displeased. "You're not making this any easier, Bryan. I'm trying to get on with my life."

"And I'm supposed to be part of the past," he murmured. He didn't like feeling obsolete...thrown out. But they walked through the place, Danni making additional suggestions: the skylight that needed to be replaced, the wood stove that should replace the old heater in the den, the brass fixtures she had in mind for the downstairs bath. At last they returned to the living room, where her gaze traveled to the fireplace.

"That shouldn't be changed at all," she said. "Promise that you won't change it. Every house has a heart, I think...and this is it."

The fireplace was fine, as far as he was concerned. But his attention was focused on Danni. He stepped toward her.

"Bryan..." Her voice held a warning.

"The time we made love," he said. "I didn't really know anything about you. But now...I do know you."

She hesitated, half swiveling as if to leave. Head bent, she seemed to be struggling with some inner turmoil. But then she turned back again, and gazed at him steadily.

"You're right, Bryan," she said. "It's different this time. There are no secrets between us anymore. But it's also too late."

"Danni, don't say that."

"I'm sorry, Bryan. It's just that—I have to change my life. I can't go on like this. Torn apart every minute... And I really *do* have to change everything. I'm even thinking about quitting my job."

She gave him a defensive glance. "I know what you're going to say next. How will I live, how will I support myself?" She paused, looking more than a little embarrassed now. "And the answer is...how the hell do I know? I'm working on it, that's all. You'd think all those years at the agency I would have thought about the future. But I didn't. The future's here. I'm pregnant, I need to change my life—and I'm completely on my own."

"You're not on your own," Bryan said.

"Yes," Danni said flatly. "I am. It's the only way, Bryan." And, with that, she left him.

CHAPTER SIXTEEN

ROBERT SERNA CLAPPED Bryan on the shoulder. ''You tried to get us the capital,'' he said. ''That's the important thing.''

''Bull,'' Bryan said. ''The money's what's important.''

Robert grinned. ''Yeah, you're right. But it's Christmas Eve. And we have to think about something else right now. Family. Festivities. That kind of thing.''

Bryan didn't have a family to speak of anymore. And he didn't have any festivities planned.

''I've been thinking of investing some of my own money,'' he said. He and Robert were inspecting one of the warehouses they planned to turn into artisan shops. There was plenty of room here, plenty of space. Just not plenty of funds.

''Sorry to tell you this,'' Robert said, ''but

your kind of money wouldn't even make a dent in this project. We need real dollars."

Real dollars as in C. J. Whitfield. Robert hadn't asked why that deal had fallen through. Maybe someday Bryan would tell him.

"Come home with me," Robert told him now. "We'll celebrate the holiday. You know Tina will be glad to see you."

Bryan liked Robert's wife, but that was no excuse to intrude on a family gathering. He said as much.

"Nonsense," Robert said. "Besides, all the neighbors will be involved tonight. Do you have anything better to do?"

The answer was no, and so half an hour later Bryan found himself drinking spiked cider and getting ready for the traditional procession through the neighborhood streets. Carrying a candle each, Robert, Tina, Bryan and other family friends went from house to house, asking for room at the inn. There was something hushed and magical about the flickering candles in the night air, and the reenactment of a drama some two thousand years old. Bryan thought how much Danni would enjoy this, and how much she would make herself a part of it.

Always Danni. Always.

They gathered more friends and neighbors as they went along, ending up back at Robert's house where, indeed, there was ''room at the inn.'' They feasted on homemade tamales, another Christmas tradition. And then there was a piñata, a bright yellow-and-blue giraffe pulled back and forth on its string until one of the children broke it wide open with a stick. Out came a shower of candy, everyone diving for all they could get.

''Too much excitement,'' Robert said as he stood beside Bryan, observing. ''And too much sugar. Tomorrow we'll all pay.''

''You think it's worth it, though,'' Bryan said.

Robert gazed at his wife and two children. ''Yeah…it's worth it.''

Another tradition was to open the presents on Christmas Eve, rather than waiting for Christmas morning. Tina handed Bryan a present of his own—a Christmas candle to take with him.

''I didn't bring you anything,'' he said.

She gave him a sisterly kiss on the cheek. ''You brought yourself, and that's enough.''

Being with the Sernas was like warming his hands before a fire. But he couldn't stay forever—he didn't want to wear out his welcome.

And so, when the family prepared for midnight Mass, Bryan bowed out.

By rights he should have gone back to his apartment, had a few becrs and hit the sack. Instead he ended up at the house. He lit the candle and put it on the mantel. He remembered Danni telling him that he shouldn't do anything to change this fireplacc, because it was the heart of the house. To him lately it felt almost as if she were the heart. Without her hcre, the place had no life.

Except for the memories. They haunted him again, a random Christmas coming to him from his childhood. Maybe he'd been eleven or so. Elizabeth had stayed late to work—again, at this house—but as soon as she'd arrived home she'd whisked him out in the car to go look at Christmas lights. She'd sung off-key carols, too. He'd pretended to hate it, but now and then hc'd joined in.

Hc kept wandering through the house, as if that would eradicate the memories. But the candle burned low, and still he remembered. He stood in the middle of the living room, and thought of the time he'd made love to Danni here. In a way they'd christened the house together. By rights she should be here with him now.

He went to the phone, intending to call her. Then he set the receiver down, before he'd even dialed her number. He blew out the candle, locked up the place and went home to his apartment. But somehow there the memories were even more potent.

THE SUGAR BEACH Country Club had gone all out for Christmas Day. Evergreen boughs laced every surface, mistletoe hung in the doorways and a giant tree decorated entirely in gold bows stood grandly in the entry. Danni thought the gold bows were on the gaudy side, but who was she to say?

Ted escorted her through the place. "They're serving rum punch somewhere around here," he said.

"I'm off rum punch for the time being."

"Right. The baby," he said. Then he paused, and Danni knew he was probably thinking about Kris...and Kris's baby. What a tangle.

"I wish we could have met somewhere else," Danni said now.

"I had to make my appearance here today. You know, keeping up appearances...can't forget that.'' He didn't sound happy about it. He got two eggnogs for them, and they went out to the patio. It was a typical California Christmas—sunny and balmy.

A woman came up to them. ''Kris, there you are at last.''

''Danni, actually. Kris's sister.''

''Oh.'' The woman retreated, her expression a familiar one to Danni. When people confused her and Kristine, they often got a resentful look, as if they felt they'd been deliberately tricked. Danni couldn't blame them, she supposed.

Ted guided her to a secluded spot. ''This is about as much privacy as we'll be allowed.''

Danni glanced around speculatively, and Ted seemed to know exactly what she was thinking.

''If you're looking for Alex Peterson,'' he said stiffly, ''she'll make sure she doesn't show when I'm here. She doesn't want to cause a real Sugar Beach scandal.''

''That would definitely be a tragedy. But why did you want to see me again, Ted? Especially after last time.''

''Look, I know that wasn't your fault,'' he said grudgingly. ''You thought I knew everything already.''

''Well, thanks for taking me off the hook.''

She sipped her eggnog, waiting for him to say what was on his mind.

"The reason I asked you here...well, it's about that fellow. The one Kris has been seeing. I guess the one you're seeing, too." He looked extremely uncomfortable. Danni felt all too uncomfortable herself.

"Ted—for the record, I'm not seeing him anymore. And Kris isn't, either. You can trust that, because Bryan's the one who told me. But you should be talking to Kris about this, not me—"

"I've tried," Ted said. "But every time we attempt a rational discussion, things just disintegrate."

Danni knew the difficulties of trying to conduct a rational discussion with her sister. But she didn't know if she could bear to stand here and talk about Bryan to Ted, of all people.

"What's he like?" Ted persisted.

Danni couldn't do this. She set down her eggnog. "Sorry, Ted—"

"Does she love him?"

This was one question not to be ignored. "She thinks she does," Danni said slowly. "But whatever she does or feels...it's always in reaction to *you,* Ted. I've been blaming her for some of the terrible stunts she's pulled—but I never quite realized until this moment how much it revolves around you.'' She eyed him severely. ''Really, Ted, you broke her heart when she found you with that woman. If she tried to hurt you in return, who are *you* to complain?''

For a moment there, it seemed as if he would try to bluster his way through. But then he gave a shrug of defeat. ''You're right, Danni. I got so mad at Kris because...well, I was trying to feel better about myself, throw all the blame on her. But it didn't work. I feel like as big a heel as ever. Maybe even worse.''

''So tell her,'' Danni urged. ''If you do it the way you did just now, you'll convince her.''

''This is Kris we're talking about, remember? Once she's decided she's been wronged, it takes a whole lot more than a few words of regret.'' He led Danni to another corner of the patio. From here they could see the emerald-green golf course stretching all the way down to the beach.

''It's beautiful,'' Danni had to admit.

''Yeah, it's beautiful. And I hate it.''

Danni glanced at him in surprise. ''But you and Kris fought so hard to join this club. You were both ecstatic the day you got in.''

''We were wrong.'' He glanced at Danni.

"Sugar Beach has been a big part of our troubles. You have to tell that to Kris for me."

"You're trying to make me into some kind of go-between."

"Right now I'll try anything." He gripped the patio railing, and stared out over the golf course. "Sure, we wanted to get into this place. And after we did...we got way too caught up in it. Trying to prove to everybody how happy and rich and successful we were. Forgetting that once upon a time, we actually knew how to have fun shopping at flea markets. And Kris...she really went after it, really tried to fit the mold. The luncheons, the charity events. Always being seen at the right place, wearing the right thing. It started to take up all her time. When we were together, it was all she talked about."

Danni listened in unwilling fascination. She'd never had quite such a glimpse into her sister's life. But, even so, she felt as if she were invading Kristine's privacy.

"Sounds like you're putting a lot on Kris," she told her brother-in-law. "Let's get to the part where *you* messed up."

"Right, right," he muttered. "I'm getting there. This is the hardest part to admit...but for quite a while there, Kris and I...let's just say things weren't going too well in the bedroom.'' He'd turned red, and Danni could see how much this was costing him. ''The problem was with me,'' he muttered. ''I couldn't seem to...well, never mind. It's supposed to happen to every guy now and then, but doesn't make it any easier. You feel like your whole self is threatened. So...when Alex Peterson paid some attention to me, and it turned out that with her I *could* function...hell, Danni. Do I have to say any more?''

''No,'' she said quietly. ''I get the picture.''

''I'm not making excuses for myself. What I did was wrong, big time. But if you could just tell Kris. If you could let her know what led up to the whole thing—maybe it'll make a difference. It's worth a shot, isn't it?''

Danni hesitated, but then she nodded. ''It's worth a try. I'll do my best, Ted.''

BRYAN WAS AT LOOSE ENDS. Christmas Day stretched out uncertainly in front of him. And so he decided to do the logical thing. He decided to wash the car.

Forget those automated systems with the rollers and the giant sponges. He preferred the old-fashioned way: your basic garden hose and a bucket of sudsy water. He was taking his time, adjusting the nozzle so it was just right, when he heard her voice.

"Bryan...it's me. Danni."

He turned and saw her. She was dressed in a tank top, faded jeans and sneakers. "Want some help?" she asked casually, coming a little closer.

He studied her for a long moment. "Sure," he said at last. "You can start over on that side. You'll find a couple of sponges in the bucket. By the way, nice try, Kris," he added.

She picked up a sponge and squeezed it. "You know it's me... Danni. I just thought we could be together...for today, at least."

"Like I said, nice try."

She sighed. Very carefully, she set down the sponge and straightened to face him. "I'm sorry, Bryan. I just wanted to be with you. How did you know?"

He almost had to smile. "I looked into your eyes. You know that old saying about the eyes being the windows of the soul? Apparently it's true. Beats me why I didn't see it before. Maybe I just kept focusing on all the wrong things. The different clothes the two of you wear. Your gestures. Your mannerisms. Superficial stuff. But now...afraid you'll never be able to fool me again, Kris."

She buried her head in her hands. ''You must be furious with me,'' she said in a muffled voice.

''Actually...no.'' What he felt was an odd lightening of spirit. ''It's really been bugging me,'' he said. ''After I found out there were two of you, not just one, I kept asking myself over and over—why hadn't I been able to tell you apart? If you think you're in love with someone, you should be able to tell. But today...I have my answer. Guess you could even say I'm grateful, Kris.''

Slowly she raised her head. ''I just wanted to be the one you loved. For a little while, at least.''

''I guess you're not giving your husband a chance,'' Bryan remarked.

She studied her clasped hands. ''He really *is* the only other man who's been able to tell us apart. But...I'm afraid, Bryan. I'm afraid it's already too late. We've both hurt each other too much.''

''Go home, Kris. You'll never know until at least you give it a try.''

She hesitated. Then she leaned over and gave him a quick kiss on the cheek. Affectionate, friendly...no implication of anything more.

"Thanks, Bryan," she said. "Thanks for everything."

After she was gone, he took his own sponge and began sudsing the car. The sense of relief stayed with him. There were still so many obstacles between him and Danni—he knew that. But he also knew the most important thing.

The woman he loved was utterly unique.

CHAPTER SEVENTEEN

"KRIS, ARE YOU HERE? Kris, hello!" Danni tapped on the door of the Sugar Beach condo, then peered through the window. Everything was dark. She was starting to get more than a little worried about her sister. She'd tried calling, but there'd been no answer. At last she'd driven over. She knocked again. Still no answer.

She walked around to the back porch. And there at last was Kristine, sitting in the starlight, her bare feet propped against the railing.

"Why didn't you answer?" Danni asked. "And why on earth didn't you show up for Christmas dinner at Mom and Dad's?"

"If you'll remember, you disowned me," Kristine said somewhat petulantly. "I figured they probably would, too, so why bother?"

"Well, just as long as you're not being dramatic about it." Danni sat beside her sister and put her own feet on the rail. The sound of the ocean waves beyond was soothing and hypnotic.

''I'll say this for Sugar Beach,'' Danni murmured. ''Sometimes it really does deliver.''

''What are you doing here?'' Kristine asked. ''I mean, if you really can't stand the sight of me and all—''

''Stop being a pill,'' Danni instructed. ''I never intended to ruin Christmas.''

''You should be more precise then. You should have said, 'I never want to see you again except for maybe two hours on Christmas Day.'''

Danni groaned. ''How long are you going to punish me?''

''I guess that's enough. But it's just awful when I can't talk to you,'' Kristine said woefully. ''I mess up even more than usual.''

''Oh, no. I don't like the sound of this. What have you done now, Kris?''

Her sister didn't say anything at first. And then she replied, ''Do you promise that you won't hate me? At least, not a whole lot?''

This really sounded ominous. ''What did you do, Kris?''

''I tried to make Bryan think I was you,'' Kristine informed her. ''But it didn't work. He looked into my eyes and he said that was how he could tell the difference. And he said he was even grateful that I'd done it, because now he knew he'd never mistake the two of us again!''

Kristine had been speaking at breakneck speed, and Danni tried to take it all in.

''Tell me again,'' she said. ''The part about Bryan—''

''He said the eyes were the windows of the soul.''

Danni smiled in the darkness. ''You really are shameless, Kris.''

''You don't hate me?'' her sister asked cautiously.

''You know I could never hate you. But if you ever, ever again pretend that you're me—''

''The charade's over,'' Kristine said in a very quiet voice.

Something in her tone made Danni believe her. ''Here's your present,'' she said, handing over a package.

Kristine tore off the paper. She'd been like that, ever since they were kids—ripping the paper and ribbons off packages in her impatience to see what was inside. Danni had always been more methodical, removing the wrapping slowly, savoring the suspense.

''What is it...?'' Kristine went to turn on the porch light so she could see. ''Oh, Danni...''

She clutched the framed photograph next to her. It was a photo from a very long time ago. It showed the two sisters at the age of fourteen, arms draped around each other, laughing into the camera. They had been at the beach, their hair and their toes full of sand.

''Get the message?'' Danni said.

''Got it.'' Kristine went into the house, reappearing a moment later with a package of her own. ''Here, Danni.''

She unwrapped it carefully. Inside was a music box. When she opened it, and the music played, two ballerinas glided across a lake of glass.

''It made me think of us,'' Kristine said. ''At least, of the way we used to be. In harmony...''

''Get real,'' Danni said fondly. ''We've been competing with each other from day one.'' She gave her sister a quick hug. ''I love my music box. But it turns out I have another present for you. A message from Ted.''

Kristine regarded her warily. ''You talked to him?''

''This very day.'' Danni faithfully repeated everything he'd told her, all the difficult parts included, but Kristine only shook her head.

''I knew we were having trouble...I mean, when you haven't had sex in a while, that's definitely a sign...but I thought Sugar Beach was what *he* wanted! And now he's saying that I became some—some Sugar Beach matron that he *despised*—"

"He's never despised you, Kris. In fact, it is pretty obvious he still loves you. Give him a chance."

"That's exactly what Bryan said," Kristine murmured.

"He's right," Danni said firmly. "Ted only told me all that because he wanted you to understand him—and forgive him."

"I have so much to think about...."

"And I'm going to leave you to it." Danni started walking toward the front of the condo, but Kristine stopped her.

"Danni, I think you really *are* going to hate me someday. Maybe pretty soon, in fact. But I just want you to know...I'm sorry for everything."

Danni came back and gave her another quick hug. "Love you, sis."

"Love you too, Danni."

DANNI HAD JUST unlocked her door when a woman came walking up breathlessly.

"So glad I finally caught you. I don't know if you remember me—"

"Of course I do," Danni said. It was one of the nurses who had tended Elizabeth McKay.

"I'm in a rush—came by earlier—but Elizabeth wanted to make absolutely sure you got this on Christmas Day, and I'm coming in just under the wire—"

Danni felt a ripple of shock. "Elizabeth?"

"Yes, at the hospital. She gave this letter to me and gave me very specific instructions. I was to keep it and then deliver it to you on Christmas Day. Poor dear lady...well, I really must go. Merry Christmas!"

Danni was left with an envelope, her name written in a wavering script on the front. Her throat tightening, she ran a fingernail under the seal, opened the envelope and scanned the letter inside. Then she read it again. And then she turned and hurried back down to her car.

BRYAN OPENED the door and observed the beautiful blonde on his doorstep. "The right sister this time," he said, drawing Danni inside.

She smiled tremulously. "Kris told me all about her latest escapade. But, Bryan—you have to read this."

He took the sheet of paper in his hand, and saw a strained handwriting. It wandered over the page as if it had cost great effort, and he took a moment to recognize it as his mother's.

Dear Danni,

You've just walked out of this hospital room, dear, and I realize there was still so much I didn't say to you. But perhaps it's better this way. You might ask yourself why I'm not writing this to my son—but you're the one who understands about the house. You understand, I'm sure, that you and Bryan are meant to live there someday. You will have to convince him of it. My dearest son bought the house because he wanted to tell me something. He wanted me to know how much he appreciated my hard work, my sacrifices for him. Will you tell him that they were never sacrifices? Will you let him know that when you truly love someone, nothing can be considered a true hardship? I loved his father. And I love him. I count my life well lived for that.

I'm very tired, Danni. And I'm very glad that I'm leaving my son in your hands. God bless the two of you, and my grandchild.

Love,
Elizabeth

Bryan didn't trust himself to speak. But he didn't need to. Danni came into his arms, and held him fiercely close.

"I'll convince you, no matter how long it takes," she said. "Your mother wanted you to stop blaming yourself for the past. She wanted you to start celebrating it instead."

He didn't know if he could ever go that far. But another weight seemed to be falling from his shoulders. It felt good to let it go.

He was still holding Danni when another knock came at the door. This time it was Kristine. She glanced from one to the other of them.

"I don't want you to think I'm making a habit of coming over here," she said quickly. "I just wanted to let you know—both of you—that I'm on my way to see Ted. I'm on my way to tell him...he's going to be a father."

"Possibly a father," Danni amended.

Kristine glanced downward. "Well, that's just the thing. There really is no doubt. The child I'm carrying...it's Ted's, all right."

Both Bryan and Danni stared at her. She seemed to quail under their gaze.

"I told you, Danni! I told you that you'd hate me very soon—after all the agony I've caused you. But if only you knew...I was on my way home from the doctor that day, so eager to tell

Ted my news. So happy to tell him that at last we were going to have a child. Only I walked in...and there he was with *her.* And after that I couldn't bear to tell him. And then I met Bryan, and it all began...." She took a quavering breath. "Go ahead and say it, both of you. Tell me that you hate me!"

"The baby's not Bryan's," Danni repeated, as if in a state of shock.

"Not even a chance. I said it because...because I felt so desperate. And I wanted something...anything to take away the pain. Only I couldn't, no matter how hard I tried. And I just ended up making everyone miserable. I'm sorry—so very sorry!" Kristine turned and hurried back out the door.

Now Bryan and Danni stared at each other. Bryan felt the last weight—the heaviest one—slip from his shoulders. He picked Danni up, whirling her around.

"Hallelujah," he said.

Danni was half laughing, half crying. "I swear I'm going to throttle my sister, really throttle her—"

"You can do that later. Right now, love, you and I are going to celebrate."

"And how exactly are we going to do that?" She smiled at him through her tears.

"We'll toast the fact that we're going to be parents. We're going to have a baby that doesn't belong to anybody but you and me."

"You really want a baby?" she asked.

"Fatherhood suddenly seems like a breeze." He kissed her thoroughly. "You're staying the night with me, Danni. You're staying forever."

"I love you, Bryan. If only you knew how much—"

"I know exactly how much. It's the same amount I love you. Immeasurable."

Now she was the one who kissed him. "Merry Christmas, Bryan."

"Merry Christmas, my love."

EPILOGUE

Christmas Eve, one year later

DANNI BALANCED Elizabeth on her hip, picking up the phone with her free hand. "Hello? Yes, Mrs. Morris...yes, I did think the marbled tile was the right choice...no, those fixtures haven't arrived yet...I'll let you know as soon as they do." Danni listened for another moment, and then, "Merry Christmas, Mrs. Morris," she said firmly. She hung up the phone.

Bryan came up behind her and kissed her ear. Elizabeth patted her father's nose.

"Hey, there," Bryan said. He scooped her into his own arms. "That lady must have called you six times already today," he told Danni.

"Seven," she said ruefully. "Let's hope that's the last." Being a general contractor was a little more complex than she'd at first imagined. But it was also the most satisfying work she'd ever done in her life. She'd left the advertising world far behind, and she didn't miss it one bit.

"Now you know what an easy client I was," Bryan told her in a solemn voice. "Don't you wish you could remodel something else for me?"

Danni glanced around her house, the one she'd fallen in love with almost from the first moment she'd seen it. She'd knocked down walls, torn up carpeting, replaced windows. But she'd left the fireplace exactly the same: plum-shaped, in pleasing red brick. The heart of the house.

One of the cats, Buster, sat atop the mantel, regally licking his paw. Dots and Oliver sat on the floor, getting ready to pounce on Buster. Meanwhile, just across from the fireplace, Kristine and Ted were dangling brightly wrapped gifts in front of Teddy Jr.

"Look at that," Kristine exclaimed in triumph. "He actually pointed. That's the present he wants."

"I don't think he was pointing," Ted said judiciously. "I think he was just grabbing."

"When will you accept it?" Kristine said in mock despair. "We have an absolutely brilliant child." She was as irrepressible as ever. She and Ted no longer lived in Sugar Beach. They'd chosen more modest environs in San Diego proper. And Kristine was no longer a society wife. Instead she'd decided she wanted to be…an airline pilot. She was attending school, taking flying lessons. Pure Kristine.

Danni watched her sister and brother-in-law. She

didn't know if the wounds had completely healed between them. Perhaps they never would. Perhaps, in a way, their marriage was stronger because of it. Who knew?

Danni tucked her hand into Bryan's arm. Now Elizabeth tried to pat *her* nose.

"I think she's discovered something new," Danni said.

"Do you think she's brilliant?" Bryan asked in a grave tone.

"Absolutely."

The phone rang again. "Oh, no," Danni said. "Mrs. Morris." But this time it was for Bryan.

"Merry Christmas, Robert," she said before handing over the receiver. Bryan and Robert talked for a moment about their project—their vision. They'd finally found the investors they needed. Everything was getting off the ground.

Bryan hung up. "Happy, love?" he murmured.

She came into his arms, their daughter nestled between them. "Very happy."

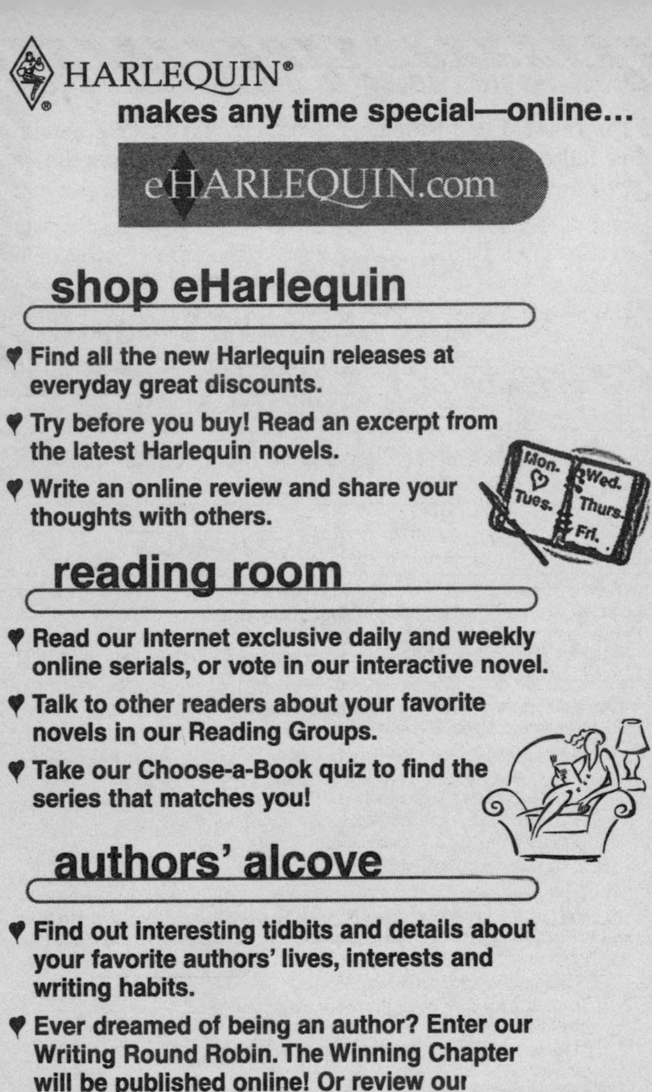
HARLEQUIN®
makes any time special—online...
eHARLEQUIN.com
shop eHarlequin
Find all the new Harlequin releases at everyday great discounts.
Try before you buy! Read an excerpt from the latest Harlequin novels.
Write an online review and share your thoughts with others.
Mon.
Tues.
Wed.
Thurs.
Fri.
reading room
Read our Internet exclusive daily and weekly online serials, or vote in our interactive novel.
Talk to other readers about your favorite novels in our Reading Groups.
Take our Choose-a-Book quiz to find the series that matches you!
authors' alcove
Find out interesting tidbits and details about your favorite authors' lives, interests and writing habits.
Ever dreamed of being an author? Enter our Writing Round Robin. The Winning Chapter will be published online! Or review our guidelines for submitting your novel.

HINTB1